LOUIS THE

Angels with L

By

AJ Howard

Illustrations are in black and white

1st Edition

Made in the USA

With Thanks:

To all rodents for their lovely faces and curly whiskers.

With Special Thanks:

Dr Ian Howard, thank you for all your assistance in making this novel successful in a beastly market. Thank you for your advice and commitment to the task, I could not have done it without you. Thank you for giving me the confidence to continue in my writing.

Cliff Cooper-Liles, thank you for grammatical assistance through various stages in the completion of this 1st edition, although I did ignore some of your crying.

Publisher information: With thanks to Amazon
Charleston, South Carolina, USA, 2011

Louis the Furred series © 1997 AJ Howard - 3 books with illustrations

All illustrations © AJ Howard 2011

subtitle Travels of a Donkey* used on next page as main title may offend

Grammatically written in UK English

All rights reserved.

No part of this publication may be reproduced, transmitted or stored in a retrieval system. Nor it is allowed to be circulated in any other form of binding other that which it is published without the prior permission of the author AJ Howard.

All characters in this book are fictitious and any resemblance to real people, living or dead is a pure coincidence.

Louis the Furred series continues 2015

IV - The Scottish Forefathers

V - The Search for Dark Matter

VI - Constellation 3.14129

Other kids stuff

Warthogs

Fat Mouse Presents series

Other stuff by AJ Howard

Travels of a Donkey*

The Asylum Years

Ten Stories High

Jimmy Riddle

Contents:	Page
Key to Creatures	6
Introduction	7-13

4 Sacred Scroll Riddles each with 6 chapters

Gone are the days of peace, a new era has begun, yet whoever meets a crushing defeat depends not on the *ONE*

1. Two Left Paws	14
2. The Crimson Factor	20
3. Crazy Kidnap	30
4. The Two Bridges	39
5. The Bottle of Waterloo	45
6. Jim's Rat-Route Revelation	57

Fitness is a factor, for those that struggle will get caught, and creating a new type of Energy will be their fault

1. Déjà vu	63
2. Jim's Injury	68
3. On Route to Kennington	76
4. Grabbed	81
5. Electro-Thought-Method	91
6. Secret Transformation	106

Can you trust living dust…?

1. Hamster Code	123
2. The Morning of the Roundish Table	131
3. The Grubby Sewers	142
4. Howard's Circus Emporium	146
5. Disguise was Wise	151
6. Oval Visions	156

Only the *ONE* of pure heart and soul will answer many questions and discover a new goal

1. Hamster Secrets	161
2. The Traitor	174
3. The *ONE* revealed	179
4. Eon's Reprieve	192
5. The Ssssylfia Test	194
6. The Awful Tower	200

The Quest Continues…

Links to Hamsterdam and Scotland	204
Author biography and book previews	212

*Note from the Author:

The creation of a written **Hamster code** sound without a solution would be, I feel, unjustified. Therefore the Wingding2 font shapes were used for some of the Living Dust chapters. These taps and scrapes can be translated, but are not similar to Morse code or Mouse code.

The full English alphabet translates in two versions:

Lower case:

a b c d e f g h i j k l m no pq r s t u v w x y z

Higher case:

A B C D E F   G H I J K L M   N O P Q R S T   U V W X Y Z

An example:

These shapes and arrows translate to spell Louis the Furred

Key to Creatures:

MICE	HAMSTERS	RATS	CROSSBREEDS
Louis	Andrew	Potty	Richard
Jane	Ken	Fruitcake	Paul
Max (the Professor)	the Collective	Truly Bonkers	Jerbil MacTaggart
Eon	MacDrid	Crazy	Howard
Jim	DaVid	Barmy	Crimson

Unpredictables	Humans
Scratchers	Cats
Round Faces	Owls
Woofers	Dogs

The Ssssylfia	Manifestation
Black and White Scratcher	Colin
Ginger Scratcher	Grimley

not all creatures will appear in every volume

INTRODUCTION

Hello, I'm **Jane,** your narrating mouse and I am back to help you through these complicated new days. After many exploits and strange twists of fate we find ourselves on route to WaterLoo; its the biggest end-of-the-tracks station of all. This one links to other countries as well as other minor towns in the only world we know, and it scares me. I have found out new things about myself since our escape and many of my first beliefs have changed. It's funny when I think of being a judge and jury or when I deserted Louis only to find out that my fellow explorers were worse leaders than him. I am trying very hard to mature but I do find myself being taken for granted too much and this upsets me. I really want to start to understand the Ssssylfia riddles more, but the further this journey takes us, the more bizarre they become. We have just been told to understand Dark Energy. A presence that is all around but cannot be seen. I do hope Louis snaps out of his misery and tries to help us find it.

Louis the Furred is still our leader, but during our time together his command and wayward tactics have caused no end of problems. Now though, as Jim and the Professor were changed into pecan nuts by a white round face, a crossbred guinea pig named Crimson has taken over command, much to Louis' regret. Crimson now says a bottle of magical juice can save our friends, so we must follow him to find it. Before Crimson Louis' flaws included a courtroom drama with the Professor over the ownership of the inventions (which Crimson now says are his!) Louis allegedly spoken to the Whites Flakes and with the Bell-Sized spider for help. Yet he is still adamant he is the *ONE* that will save us from Andrew and Ken. He believes too much in Sacred Scrolls and is becoming a liability in our quests. This once proud mouse has turned nasty. Maybe I shouldn't be too hard on him. He did lead our escape and I was the one that voted in his favour with regard to naming our new world.

Max, or the Professor as he likes to be called, is still a funny old mouse. He has proved time and again that he is a cheat and a liar. The inventions that he said were his and won a court case over may not have been his after all. He lies out of greed and yet, as a comrade from our sawdust prison days, he still belongs to the fellowship of Louis' World. The problem is I don't trust him at all anymore. I wonder what other lies or dangers lurk in this strange new world. He has of course made one fundamental error. Both he and Jim were greedy at Chalky Farm and have been transformed into pecans. If he was such a clever mouse why did he allow this to happen? His quest though is different to ours. He is searching for his stepbrother Paul and this may jeopardise our Dark Energy aspirations. He has a wicked side: I remember he stabbed Jim once at Cam's Den to scare some scratchers away. Yet he did get captured by other scratchers at High Gate and he understood Eon's desire to stay with his new friends. But now he, like Jim, is in danger and he, like Jim, needs to rely on us to save his life.

Eon is a mouse not much older than me. He is a tough and selfish creature. But at last he has begun to fulfil his destiny. He is the only one from the original escape crew who knows what he wants. He has now left our guidance to move to High Gate and join the Rodent Army in a bid to fight against the hamster regime. If there is one thing against him, it would be the naïve nature that he displays. He says he has a clawless scratcher named Grimley as an ally. But Jim reckons this flaw in his trust will cost him his life. Don't get me wrong, I salute Eon for trying to find a future but worry that he has chosen the wrong path. He always does what he wants and isn't very good at following discipline. He has a lovely temperament when he is around us but he does come across as a bit thick. I hope this isn't really his nature at all and that his new friends help him to be the warrior that he thinks he is. It must be strange to have rats as comrades. I do wonder if he really knows what he is letting himself in for.

Jim is still my favourite mouse. He has the ability to turn bizarre events into believable events. He can escape danger and through his visions, which contradict the Sacred Scrolls, he has inadvertently proved that many of them are false. He is still too naïve to lead the group though. When he was caught in two dreams at the same time in Cam's Den it was definitely very strange and not the sort of thing that would happen to me. When he became trapped inside a chocolate machine and understood Louis' mouse code, it was impressive. Yet his escape was, as usual, complimented by an exaggerated tale involving a young bee and his interpretation of events always has to include crocodiles and alligators. But, his foolish wishes being granted by a white round face have left him and the Professor trapped inside pecan shells and only with Crimson's and our help will we find an antidote to the spell that has been cast upon them.

Crimson is our newest ally as we search for a solution to Jim's and the Professor's predicament. He is the same age as Louis but is a small crossbred guinea pig and mouse. If I ever get to tell any of my seven sisters that I was following orders from a guinea pig only twice my size they'd have thought I was mad. What a funny world this is becoming. Louis suggested that Crimson has Napoleonic tendencies and is linked to the Ssssylfia prediction that one of us may die. Crimson has told me of many of his adventures and he has opened my eyes to the size of this world. Yet for him to be a leader is quite odd, you see, he likes to work alone. He mentioned that he'd never seen the Ssssylfia before yet he as been across the Great Sea and told me tales of Rodent Armies and hamster populated cities. His biggest flaw though is he lacks the ability to communicate properly and only time will tell if this will be his downfall.

As Volume three begins

our future is still uncertain

as many roads lead to dangers

and these risks may end our lives…

> Gone are the days of peace.
> As a new era has begun, yet
> whoever meets a crushing defeat
> depends not on the *ONE?*

1. Two Left Paws

Originally we had planned to start the day trying to understand Dark Energy, and I remember Jim had a defining belief in what it was, but I too believe I know the answer and it's different to his. Alas I think none of us can truly define what Dark Energy is fully, nor indeed do we have any actual proof of the whole theory or idea which we know is just that, a theory and an idea.

Jim, our complaining friend, now seems an integral part of our team. Yet his visions and his senses contradict the Sacred Scrolls at every turn. In an error of judgement both Jim and the Professor have been changed into pecans by a mysterious white round face. Bizarrely, this round face seemed to praise and worship Jim but now we can see the beast was just toying with him. It appears that this round face tricked both Jim and the Professor and now only the magical DM juices can save our friends.

Crimson suggests DM is a substance known as Dark Matter. I wonder if this is related in any way to the Dark

Energy that we seek. For they are both dark and tricky to find. Surely to call them Invisible Energy and Invisible Matter would be more accurate. Does it matter? Well, I suppose not really, at least not yet anyhow.

We are being led to WaterLoo by an arrogant crossbreed. He is a left pawed guinea pig and mouse and his full name is Crimson Pigs. As his name indicates, he is a strong reddish colour but unlike his name suggests, he is quite small. He's not as tiny as us mice, but compared to hamsters he is like a dwarf. It's odd for us to be following a new leader. Louis is ironically left pawed too and had been quite a good leader really. I know we've had our ups and downs, but overall even Jim thinks Louis has lead us well. But those days, at least at present, are over. I wonder if it is relevant that left pawed creatures become great leaders; I guess only time will tell.

We have a new mission. We must forget the Dark Energy mystery for the time being and try to locate the Dark Matter magical juice instead. The ingredients are unknown, yet the powers of this liquid are fantastic. The Professor would, I think, be the best to inform you of what the DM juices can do. Alas he is trapped inside a pecan shell, so the tale of our quest and the answers you seek, at this stage anyway, will have to come from me…

Crimson believes that the DM juices are located near a bridge of some description. He hasn't told me or Louis this. I overheard him mumbling to himself about it. He tells us nothing, you see. If he was the kind of rodent to tell us what was happening then great. But this Crimson character makes up his own mind. He does what he does well, but what he doesn't do well, is communicate.

Anyway, we're on one of the mechanical beasts and heading towards WaterLoo because a riddle set by the Ssssylfia suggests we go there. And we are being led by Crimson (who had never seen the Ssssylfia before) to find a rat named Crazy who may be able to help. Crazy eh? Oh yeah, before I forget, we are all carrying nuts. I'm carrying Jim (a pecan), but because he's still slightly tubby, his whiskers were caught in the transformation process so they stick out a bit. We can hear him whining and complaining sometimes, so he's definitely alive. We did try to crack the shell once but the amount of abuse we got from him about the pain, well, we decided to leave him in there. Louis is carrying our prison-break buddy Max (also a pecan). Max's preferred title (as he is big-headed) is the Professor and he claims, even after all that's happened, that the sack of inventions are his. But logic would suggest that the crimson-coloured sack containing the tablets belongs to Crimson Pigs and not the Professor. Anyway, the Professor grabbed this sack and it inadvertently became jammed inside the pecan nut too- much to Crimson's annoyance. And finally, Crimson is carrying a hazelnut that he thinks is Paul, Max's stepbrother. Although Louis thinks it may be a different Paul or indeed a different rodent altogether, because it is a different type of nut.

So there you have it... Oh no, I forgot something. Crimson has got the Rodent Key too. He stole this from Ken Archdeacon and the Collective. These hamsters lost in a game of Words with Jim and the Professor on Hamstered Heath, but were outfoxed by Crimson posing as a hamster named RedBush. Yes, it does seem a little far-fetched and complicated, but if you know how the story goes, then you will know how it could end. The hamsters have given us a deadline to meet at the King's church at 12pm Friday. Why? They will offer a kidnap-style showdown where we will get Richard- who is possibly the 2nd in line to the throne of Jerboa (if it is Richard) and in return they want the Rodent Key that Crimson stole from them. Of course, Crimson doesn't want to give the key to these hamsters, nor does he expect that Richard is in their custody. Richard incidentally may not be 2nd in line to the throne of Jerboa and he may not exist at all! The Sacred Scrolls state Richard is a crossbred gerbil and mouse and a vital cog in rodent futures, but he is not the *ONE* that will save us all. I have never seen Richard and nor has Louis, or Jim or Max for that matter, so in reality, these hamsters could bring along any old rodent and we wouldn't have a clue if it were him or not.

So, there you have it. Sorry, I'm repeating myself. It's time I think to look for Crazy. My two left pawed leaders are clashing already. I just seem to be the go-between these days. Anyway, Louis has just woken up and Crimson has started to annoy him already...

I was standing shoulder to shoulder with Louis on the rear bumper of the mechanical beast and Crimson was perched by the edge gazing into the blackness. He wore his colour-coded hat and scarf and looked like a hero. He also wore a charismatic smirk that never left his face and he seemed to look down on Louis as though he were a loser or an underachiever. I didn't have the heart to tell Louis what I thought Crimson looked like as I could see in his eyes that he hated our new colleague, but worse than that, he hated being told what to do.

As we approached WaterLoo the beast stopped and all the lights went out. We stared into the tunnel and waited. As if on cue, out of the blackness the Ssssylfia appeared; this strange manifestation then hovered over and spoke to us.

Again Crimson seemed shocked by its appearance until Louis knocked him down a peg or two. "This Ssssylfia ghost only speaks to mice, its there for our benefit not yours."

"Rubbish," replied Crimson. "It speaks to me not you."

I interrupted the arguing fools (who were leading the expedition for the salvation of Jim and the Professor) with what I thought was quite a relevant question, "What does the Ssssylfia mean by DM DM?"

"I know what the DM DM is," smirked Crimson, "ask Louis, see if he knows."

"I don't, sorry," he mumbled.

"Well it's Dark Matter! Actually it's Dark Matter Does Matter if you want to get technical, but where the DM is, I'm not so sure. Crazy will know the location though. That's why we're going to WaterLoo, to find Crazy."

"Whatever," sighed a miserable, dejected Louis. He knew now that he had met his match, as Crimson was by far a more experienced leader than he'd ever be…

2. The Crimson Factor

The scene was set and the task had become real. As usual, Jim's foolish acts, along with the Professor's, had set up our new mission. We knew WaterLoo was where we had to go but with Crimson leading us, things weren't as cut and dried as all that...

"I overheard you talking to Jane earlier about something crazy, there's no escape from my ears," growled Louis.

"You do realise we call that eavesdropping where I come from. Look, you don't want to annoy me you know, I'm your link to this magic juice."

"So, what kind of juice is it Crimson? What are the ingredients, do you know?" I asked.

"Jane, I believe I know of some of its flavours," stated Crimson with authority in his voice. "It is written that it tastes of freshly squeezed tomato juice and there is an unpredictable named Nelson who prepares an odd concoction that goes into it. I don't know what this would be off hand. It is written that this unpredictable wears no earrings, that he fluked the potion, the liquid or the juice, which ever way you want to put it."

"This is fun isn't it," I said, "I think it's quite nice not having Jim and the Professor moaning at us all the time. To think that we hold them in these little, but heavy pecans is funny really. If I ever met any one of my seven sisters again they'd never believe that so many mice get turned into pecans and put into pies in Mor's Den and at Chalky Farm too. They'd probably think that I'd lost my mind. Well it doesn't sound very realistic does it Crimson… Crimson! Oh don't fall asleep on me when I'm talking, I hate that, that's the kind of thing Jim used to do." But he had gone to sleep and so had Louis.

I thought about talking to Jim as he couldn't run away could he, but no, I too decided it was about time for me also to take forty winks… I leaned my body against Louis and drifted away into dreamland.

"Jane are you sleeping?" asked Crimson. He had the same annoying trait that Louis had. He was lying face forwards but worse, he was talking to me with his eyes closed.

"Well I was trying to, what do you want?"

"Do you not want to ask me anything? Have you got no longing for knowledge?" smirked the arrogant half-breed.

"Louis always said that you were modest. You like talking about yourself. I knew in my soul that it wouldn't be long before you started heaping your tales of woe upon us. Don't get me wrong, by the way. I mean it in the nicest way."

"Modest. He said I was modest? The slime."

"Well?"

"Well what?"

"Well why not tell me about yourself. I know your name but where do you come from? I know I was born and raised in London but I can tell from that accent of yours that you're not English."

"I come from France, it's a long story this, do you want to hear it?"

"Well just feed me with fragments please."

"Right, I was exiled by a mouse named Louis. Not your Louis a different one. This one was on the throne of France at the time. I was banished to a town called Elbow but I escaped. Alas I now work alone as some of my so-called best friends deserted me in my moment of need. It is written that loyalty is the most precious quality but I believe these allies were treacherous. After I returned I went on a mission to capture the notorious Belgian bun stealer. He had been seen in the region of Brussels. I had crossed the border into Belgium by this time. I believed he was a regular with the Brussels based corporation known as the Sprouts. They were a group of highly intelligent rats that used to disguise themselves as tiny cabbages. They used to pillage the hamster controlled supermarkets. One of these Sprouts unfortunately had a sweet tooth. He was keen on the taste of the sticky bun, this of course being the Belgian bun."

"So why did you come to England at all?"

"Well Jane, because of Colonel Paul Richard. He is a two-named rodent. He is known as Paul to most rodents but Richard to hamsters as he is a double agent. He sent me a message saying that Crazy had been seen in London. Crazy is just a nickname for this rat, it means he'll do anything to get what he wants. You see Crazy is crazy."

"Is Crazy English?"

"No. Crazy is Belgian, I told you that!" moaned Crimson as he started to pace up and down. "Some of the Sprouts who trained with him at the same time said he used to do mad things. A rat named Barmy said that Crazy used to come top in everything. Crazy eh? Another rat named Loopy, though, was the only one he trusted. You see, Loopy was his best friend until he was eaten by a scratcher. Rumour has it that Crazy once had a fight with Truly Bonkers, a brutish rat with eyebrows that met in the middle, but as it happens nothing came of it."

"So where are these Sprouts now then?"

"They're working in the sewers near Oxon Circus with the Rodent Army. I know it sounds mad but that's what they were trained to do.

Truly Bonkers is a good leader in the High Gate division. He gets on really well with uneducated rodents, almost to the point of comradeship. But these Sprouts are more than just spies."

"So where does this rodent with two names think Crazy is?"

"He's not sure, but as a hunch he reckons that Crazy knows where this scientist Nelson lives. I know none of you mice like unpredictables but this one's different. He has grown his own whiskers, they cover most of his face."

"So you're saying that our mission is to find a rat with a silly name, to assist us in finding this magical juice for our trapped friends."

"Yes... we must find Crazy."

"Okay, I think I understand."

I have to admit (just like Jim's) Crimson's tales of woe and self belief sounded somewhat exaggerated. I admit I have met rats that camouflage themselves too. They were little cabbages, so maybe it wasn't too bizarre to think that Crazy could be from the elite task force known as the Sprouts.

"Is Crazy the one that knows where the bottle is?" I asked Crimson.

"Yes... look, this mechanical beast is steadily creeping towards the end-of-the-tracks; we have to get off here."

Crimson woke Louis and I stuffed both the Professor and Jim into my pockets and followed. Crimson led us to the main station area. It was enormous. We've never seen anything like it.

Inside the place was teaming with unpredictables most of whom wore earrings. Crimson then pointed to an enormous mechanical beast that had brought him here from Brussels. He said that these were similar to the beasts in the underground tunnels and apart from their size, the only difference was that they travelled over ground.

"This over ground beast," said Crimson pointing at it, "would then scoot through a dark tunnel which goes under the Great Sea."

Louis yawned and decided to join in the conversation. "So the over ground beast can travel under ground too? Weird. You're not telling me you've been under the Great Sea are you? But, how?"

"These unpredictables aren't as stupid as you think Louis. You see that one there in the peaked cap." He pointed towards an unpredictable with no earrings and what looked like slightly greying whiskers. "That one's the driver. These beasts need these unpredictables to make them work. These beasts cover the world not just this country. Louis, how many countries do you think there are in the world?"

"Err...well... three," he mumbled.

"Three! Ha! Ha! Which three are they?"

"Well London's one. The country to the right of the Great Sea is two and Scotland is three."

"Louis, there are more than three countries you fool! My, my, Louis! I thought you knew how large the world was. It's vast. It's filled with hundreds of countries and hundreds of seas. There are places that are just deserts. There are places that are just forests. There are volcanic areas. There are areas over populated with unpredictables. The East holds lots of fantastic stories. Louis oh Louis, I though you knew. Maybe you're just a minnow in this world. A nobody. If you don't understand what's going on you've got no chance." Crimson sulked by the Great station's escalators that over looked these mechanical beasts.

"But I know we need to find Dark Energy. It's just, well, complicated you see," muttered Louis.

"You have to understand everything else before you can even think about Dark Energy. You don't know enough! You'd better just rescue your friends and then succumb to a nothing lifestyle; or you could decide to expand your mind. Learning is everything. It is written that faith is the key to all doors."

"Is this door we seek in this unpredictable's home, the door of faith?" I asked.

"Yes. It is the safe of faith that we must open using the Rodent Key and that's why the hamsters want it. A key to a safe containing DM juices is a valuable key indeed. Now come with me."

Crimson led the way and we followed. I turned to Louis and he looked sad. He though that he was a failure. To us he was a leader but to Crimson he was a nobody. It's funny that. A small team in its own world is the best around. Yet as soon as you enter the real world, this large, uninviting, cruel place, everything becomes scary. Louis I think understands this now. He was blind to the truth because no one had taken the blinkers away from his eyes. It is written that ignorance is bliss, but truth hurts like nothing else on earth. We ran down some large steps underneath the station. Crimson was dictating as usual. It wasn't the same with him in charge. He asked us to do exercises before we went into this building. He said it was important that we stretched and limbered up before we jumped into the cauldron of death.

"Are you sure this is the way?" chirped Louis. He seemed to have pepped up.

"Shhh! Don't talk to me in that tone," moaned Crimson.

"What?"

"Shhh!"

"Look, this is my ball game, I'm in charge," snapped Louis.

"Louis, this is no game." Crimson stared him in the face. Louis started to think of Jim and how he mimicked his complaining ways.

"Which way now?" I asked. We could see a parade of unpredictables running down the steps where we were. We were sitting in the middle and but as Crimson attempted to lift one of the pieces of concrete up, his hat and scarf fell off and tumbled down the steps.

"Hey you two, over here, lend me a paw will you? Now where's my sack...? Oh yeah... Damn..."

"I suppose so," mumbled Louis. His spirit had gone. He was developing an attitude, which, as any mouse knows, is a worrying problem.

I stared at Crimson and said, "I can't help you as I've got the Professor and Jim in my pockets and they weigh enough as it is."

"It doesn't matter look, I've done it." He pulled the loose stone away, grabbed his hat and scarf and led us under the station.

It was very dark inside. The Professor had the sack of inventions in the shell with him so we didn't have access to a Max-Lantern.

CLUNK!

Crimson walked straight into a loose beam and it knocked him to the floor. He then began whining, "Oh my head, my head."

We stopped scampering after that and lay motionless watching the world drift by whilst trying to keep still. But more importantly, we kept quiet and strove to listen out for anything that would lead us to this hungry rat…

3. Crazy Kidnap

After a while we could hear a munching sound. It seemed like it was coming from underneath one of the shops. You see, as this station was so large certain businesses used the influx of rushing unpredictables to their advantage. If they could sell quick easy items to these fools they'd make a decent living. One of the shops was a coffee house, another was a magazine shop, you know, newspapers, books and things. But the one we heard the noises coming from was a pastry shop. An unpredictable by the name of Rundle had set up a snack bar. It was the kind of place to have a cake, a tart or a sticky bun... and now you see the relevance. The closer we got to this shop the louder the munching got. Crimson said the shop was built centuries ago and its floor was made of wood. These floorboards had a slither of light creeping through each joining crack. This light made it possible for us to see what was going on.

"Over there look, by the vent," I whispered, pointing.

"That's Crazy I think," whispered Crimson.

"Why?" asked Louis.

"Why what?" asked Crimson.

"Why's it crazy that Jane's seen a vent?"

"No! You don't understand, that's Crazy you know, Crazy, C-R-A-Z-Y!"

"What are you talking about?"

"He says it's Crazy the Belgian bun stealing rat, he is part of the Sprouts gang," I answered.

"What? You've lost me," mumbled Louis as he turned towards us and sighed.

"Basically we need Crazy's help to find the unpredictable who owns the faith safe. Without Crazy we'll never find him," answered Crimson.

"So how did you know Crazy would be here?"

"Because Rundle's Grub Haven is known all over Europe for its flavoursome grub. I had a hunch that Crazy wouldn't be able to resist Rundle's pastries. We'll have to offer him all the Belgian buns he can eat if we're to find this unpredictables' lair. Look, I'll try to reason with him and you two stay here."

We watched as Crimson crept slowly towards Crazy but then a horrible thing happened, Crimson jumped on him. He grabbed Crazy by the whiskers and hoisted him into a black bag. He giggled and dragged the shell-shocked rat back towards us.

"Urrr! Urrr! What's happening?" screamed Crazy.

"Look, I object to you handling him like that," growled Louis.

"You're not in the position to object. I'm in charge, come with me..."

Crimson led us out through the same hole in the station steps. He then struggled along with Crazy who was still cursing and seething. "Let... me... out... I say?"

Myself and Louis took up the rear. Louis was very chatty. I guess he knew that because Crimson was small he was over aggressive. I think it was a size thing. He was trying to prove that just because he was small it didn't mean he was weak.

"He shouldn't drag Crazy like that it's mean," sighed Louis.

"Yeah, I agree." I was happy that Louis wasn't pleased with Crimson's behaviour because nor was I. And whilst Louis was moaning to me, we could see Crimson interrogating and torturing Crazy ahead of us. It was awful.

"I can't wait for the day when we can say goodbye to this guinea pig," squeaked Louis. "I realise that he's put me in my place. Maybe I was becoming too big for my boots. It's funny, I kind of miss Jim. The babyish argumentative conversations are lacking you know. Still, that Crimson, he's been around a bit hasn't he, although I bet he exaggerates the truth too much.

He's not stupid though. He's quite clever. I just think that maybe his problem is that he's trying too hard and torturing that poor rat isn't exactly good is it? I disagree with his tactics and it makes me sad. You remember that sometimes Jim gets all bossy and arrogant, well that's the kind of face Crimson shows. Do you remember when we saw him with those hamsters? I bet he argued with Ken that he should be RedBush, but well, that's all water under the bridge now."

"Louis! Louis! Crazy says we need to go under the bridge, where the water is, how did you know?" moaned Crimson.

"I didn't."

"But you just said it, didn't you?"

"Yes… but you didn't listen to the context of the sentence. It was about something else. Anyway, it was my conversation so it was none of your business."

"But I heard you say my name."

"That's because I was talking to Jane about you."

"What! About my size no doubt!"

"No, about your attitude," moaned Louis.

"But I haven't got one."

"Oh but you have."

"Liar," squeaked Crimson.

"I'm not lying."

Then Crimson turned his attention to me, "Have I an attitude problem Jane?"

"Yep."

"So you two mice are ganging up on me, so what. I can handle it. I'm cool."

"It doesn't really matter as that just you being you," I argued.

"Well, that's all right then, I think," Crimson muttered back.

"So, why are we going under the bridge?" Louis asked.

"Crazy reckons the unpredictable has a base there, under the water, under the bridge."

"Is he truly reliable or bonkers, like his name suggests."

"Truly Bonkers may well be here with this unpredictable, yes."

"What?" quizzed Louis.

"Try listening," argued Crimson.

"Oh never mind," sulked Louis. He didn't have a clue what Crimson was saying as Crimson didn't communicate very well. "Can you tell me what's going on Jane?"

"Sure." I told Louis Crimson's tale of exile and escape and his investigations in Brussels.

"So, Crimson, you're nothing but a part-time detective correct?"

"I'm full-time! The Belgian authorities have liaised with the European Federation of Rodents (EFR) actually. But of course you don't know where that is do you. The EFR are based in

Hag's Den in HollyLand. This is the home of a wizened old hag that runs rodent law. You see, now that you're out of your prison your eyes and mind are noticing that all rodents are seeking recognition. You're not the only group of mice to have escaped you know. The underground network of London is teaming with them. I suggest you get to know where you're from before you even consider to locate the ONE and join the elite on the Dark Matter expedition. Certain aspects of your character say to me that you have what it takes Louis, don't throw that away in a simple argument with me. I'm just a messenger. If you want to join the elite team you must prove your worth."

"Well, I'll try," mumbled a sad and dejected Louis.

"If you try, make sure you give it your best shot. It is written that if you give 100% every time you'll be everything you've ever wanted."

"Yeah I've read that one, I know it off by heart."

"Then maybe you are gonna be a true hero one day."

Louis looked me in the eyes. He was so focused. I remember him telling me once that he wasn't doing this to be a hero. He didn't want that noose of hero hanging around his fluffy neck. He wanted only the belief and support and recognition of his friends and all the other rodents that he did what he did for them. It's true he wanted to be famous, but as a warrior fulfilling a worthwhile cause. He said there was no point to his life if he had to gamble with peanuts and if his life centred around buying and selling to make a profit in something that wasn't relevant to the success of his species. But that's a typical answer for him. Louis will always be a hero in my eyes whether he proves the true meaning of Dark Energy, or discovers the ingredients of Dark Matter, or locates the *ONE* or not. The things he's achieved so far are the things that will be remembered by me forever.

"Look Louis, over there." Crimson pointed to a floating platform that led out onto the river. "Come on let's go, there's no time to lose."

Crimson dropped the black bag carrying the injured rat and Crazy rolled out of it in front of us. He was bruised but licked his lips as he scampered towards WaterLoo again. I ran over towards this sad, pathetic rat and hugged him. I was upset by the way Crimson treated him and I wanted to tell him that mice are not like that.

"Are you okay?" I asked him.

"Yeah. Thanks. I'm hurting a little. I think a sugar rush would sort me out so I'm heading for Rundle's Grub Haven. Oooo, yummy," he said, as he licked his chops.

"Are you really going now?" I asked.

"Yes I must, I warn you though, watch your back regarding that small rodent. He's meant to be on our side but he treated me like scum. Listen to me mouse, this is very important… that Jerbil MacTaggart and those Sacred Scrolls are not real. Nor are the drawn on Rat-Routes. This knowledge is secret and may cost you your life."

"What are you saying? Are the legendary beliefs all lies? How can that be?" I was confused and distraught.

"I am a team member of the Sprouts division. I am also the guardian of the faith safe. I shouldn't have told Crimson it's whereabouts, but well, actually I lied. There are very few camouflaged rats in London like me and we are all looking for the *ONE*. Many brainwashed uneducated rats live in the sewers and scavenge for food. The hamsters have banished them to slavery and my brothers have evolved to become two-faced. Listen to me, sewer rats and any type of crossbreed cannot be trusted. These rodents are all keen on circus acts, watch your back as they will double-cross you. The biggest problem with London is the hamster control. Rats, gerbils, guinea pigs and jerboas have become slaves, yet their greatest fear is mice. They are converting all mice into pecan nuts and eating them. The stronger the hamsters become, the more they have control you see. The *ONE* that we all seek can outwit them," said Crazy.

"But what of our friends in these pecans?" I asked him as I pointed to my buddies trapped inside the shells.

"Watch your back. Believe in your friends and they will begin to believe too. Use DM juices to rescue them. Use the Rodent Key that Crimson has to open the faith safe which hides this liquid. Be very cautious though, as a scratcher hides within the chamber. I will head for EFR soon to inform them of Crimson's treachery. Keep this one safe," he stroked Jim's shell and ran off alone towards the station.

"Don't listen to that rat Jane, he's not all there in the head," moaned Crimson. He wasn't happy that I was talking to him but at least he allowed it. I guess Louis wouldn't have allowed it, so in a way I was lucky.

I waved in the direction of Crazy but he didn't look round at all as he disappeared from sight. And then Crimson led us towards the floating platform. I followed, but out of disrespect Louis was lagging behind as usual.

4. The Two Bridges

"Okay I'm coming, oh wait..." Louis seemed to twitch and then started twisting his head around as though he were looking for something, "Where's Crazy gone?"

Now here is another dilemma: whether to tell Louis the whole truth or just the parts I think he'll want to hear. I decided on the latter, to hide the full truth, but I was worried it might be a mistake. I decided to babble at him, give him a long winded answer that wasn't really an answer at all. It's the sort of thing he does to me, so now it was my turn. I said, "Oh he's gone on the trail of some more buns. He told me that I'd find him where the sun sets every night. A place where, when you look out over the horizon, his face will glisten across the ocean and when the motion of the waves say goodbye his memories will stay awake in the glowing night sky....."

"So what does that mean?"

"It means he's going home soon, to a land across the Great Sea."

We all scampered along the floating platform. I pushed the Professor and Jim deep into my pockets in case they fell into the freezing murky river known as the Thames.

"Why do you reckon that this river's called the Thames Louis?" I asked.

"Well, this is no ordinary large stream of natural water. It contains some sea water."

"But why Thames? What does Thames mean?" I asked him again.

"I believe the Thames has a link to hamsters. It is very like the Scottish word for home which is hame. Two Scottish homes would be two hames. I think that a lazy hamster who lived in two hames decided that rather than cross the river that split his two hames he'll own that section of the river too. Thus making a bridge to two hames. Also Thames is an anagram of hamster, well of hamste and the last letter R must come from the title i.e. R-iver; so it must be true. So what's your theory?"

"I haven't got one Louis," I replied.

"How about you Crimson, what do you think?"

"Louis, rather than talk about useless things let's climb down these ropes and swim to that flashing buoy over there." Crimson pointed to a life buoy about thirty feet away.

"Yeah okay," we all replied.

We swam towards it but the hamster river had strong currents with dark currants in it. I was hit at least three times by a wayward blackberry. We made it to the buoy quite quickly. There was another rope hanging around the buoy. Crimson then said he was going to take a little swim underwater in an attempt to locate the unpredictable's Den.

"Isn't it a bit odd that this unpredictable lives in the river, Louis?" I asked.

"Some of these unpredictables have odd habits."

"But don't you think it's a tad fishy that Crimson hasn't tried to double cross us yet?"

"Yeah, it worries me a bit," sighed Louis. Then we saw a few bubbles and the soggy head of our new leader emerged from the depths. "Oh look here he comes now."

"Did you find it?" I asked.

"Yeah it's definitely down there," said Crimson, "I think it's an old riverboat with the word Yale on it. I wonder what kind of cargo it used to have?"

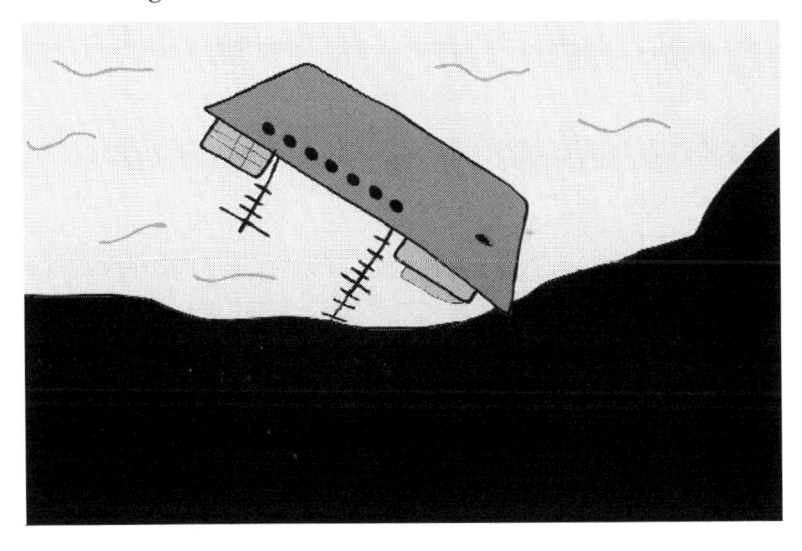

"I've heard of it. Isn't that the brother boat of Harvard that was sunk by a mad unpredictable in the Great Sea?"

"Well Louis it was enormous and upside down so who knows." We all took three deep breaths and one at a time we dived under the water heading for the boat. Crimson led the way. I'm just so pleased that I learnt to swim when I was young; I never thought it would be a skill that would one day prove to be important. Luck I guess. So many of the other mice where I grew up pretended to swim, but couldn't. They thought it was a joke, but if they were with me today they'd realise it wasn't. We made it quite quickly to the submerged boat. It took about forty seconds of intense swimming. It was almost pitch black under the water and the only way we managed to stay together was by holding onto a piece of rope that Crimson had pulled off the buoy. He led us into an airlock and we breathed again.

"This bottle will probably be in the faith safe situated on the bridge," Crimson said.

"On the bridge!" screamed Louis.

"Yes, on the bridge is what I said dopey, you don't listen do you?"

"What? Why on earth did you get us down here then? Are you trying to double cross us then kill us off? Yes! Yes! That's it isn't it? You're in league with this unpredictable aren't you? We're gonna die down here aren't we? You're mad! I hate you! I hate you!" Louis screamed. He collapsed in front of me and his head bobbled under the water again. "Why? All I want to know is why?"

"What are you talking about?" asked a confused Crimson.

"Murder this is and no one will know, how could you?" sighed Louis.

"You're babbling Louis! Louis! Snap out of it!" Crimson went right over to him and slapped him in the face.

"Don't you hit me!"

"What's got into you?"

"Oh that's right, plead ignorance!"

"Come on quickly, let's get to the bridge," Crimson shouted again. Louis looked sad but followed anyway, as did I. We swam under the water again and through a porthole on the starboard side. We swam past some upside down stairs and reached the wheelhouse of the boat.

Suddenly Crimson yelled out "Damn!"

"What's wrong?" I asked.

"It's wrong!" We watched as Crimson pulled picture after picture off the wall. "It's wrong. Damn!"

"What is?" I asked. I was more confused than usual. I felt all right in my mind but Louis, who was once so controlled, had lost the plot earlier and was raving about Crimson killing us and I didn't know what to think anymore.

"It's not here," squeaked Crimson again.

There was a tiny airlock in the wheelhouse and we all swam towards it. We breathed again. In the unpredictable's language this area was called the bridge, and Louis became sheepish and looked embarrassed, now realising he'd misunderstood. He thought Crimson had led us to this submerged boat to kill us off, as any mouse knows a bridge spans across a river not under it. But, because of Crimson's useless communication skills we were at a bridge now, but the bridge of the boat where its captain would sail, steer and command from.

I looked towards Louis for inspiration but he was silent and embarrassed. I turned to Crimson and he just stared at an upside down picture on the wall and started moaning again, "See that, it was meant to be behind that and it's not. Crazy lied!"

"You've lost me," mumbled Louis.

"Hang on, look, over there!" Crimson pointed to another picture, this one had a large concrete pillar sticking high into the sky with four giant scratchers guarding it. He then pointed to an empty bottle cellar under the steering column of the ship. "You see it?"

"What's going on in your head? Why are we looking at a picture of Scratcher Square?" asked Louis. "That's on the north bank of this river."

"Yes that's it, we must go there!" shrieked Crimson.

"Why?" I asked. But Crimson kept his thoughts to himself as usual...

5. The Bottle of WaterLoo

Louis looked confused and I didn't blame him. Crimson was good at what he did but his lack of communication meant we didn't know at all what was going on. We all swam to the other side of the river and scampered towards the pillar. Fortunately the giant scratchers weren't real, just statues. We watched Crimson picked at a loose stone and we followed him in.

It was odd inside and all we saw was a daunting spiral staircase with hundreds of steps leading upwards. After ages and ages of walking we reached the top and entered the library chamber. Along the walls in great racks there were books about every species of animal and about every country. Crimson then pointed to a round ball on a tabletop and called it our planet. He said this was a replica version of the world we lived on.

"Our planet is about 40,075 miles in circumference," gloated Crimson, "and London makes up about 1/1000 of it. The universe though is infinite as it has no end. Let me explain: as a rough guess I would say the universe is ten billion times bigger than our planet. And just for the record, Dark Matter makes up 85% of the universe, so finding it in this library should be easy."

He then went on to say that the library was the property of Nelson (an unpredictable with greying whiskers). He told us that nearly all of the unpredictable's who study the world have whiskers. I guess we could assume this was a good sign then, as we had them too.

Crimson noticed a safe at the top of a large ladder. Without speaking to us he sneaked towards it and began to climb. Myself and Louis were unfortunately distracted, as we were watching a large tortoiseshell scratcher that had entered the premises unannounced.

"Crimson, we'd better be cautious, there's a scratcher in here with..... where is he? Jane, where is he?" whispered Louis.

"Look Louis, he's up there." I pointed to him struggling above us, unfortunately the mottled scratcher had noticed too and was licking its chops. Then disaster struck. We could do nothing but watch him, he put the key in the lock and turned it, then disaster, he slipped. The door of the safe of faith swung open and knocked him into the clutches of the furry fiend. We watched as he was eaten alive in front of us. The fool. If only he'd told us what he was doing. If only.

"This is disgusting," sighed Louis, "never in my life have I witnessed a comrade die in such a horrible way. I guess we'll have to inscribe his tombstone with the words: Crimson Napoleon Pigs lies here today. He was a small friend with a big heart. If he'd learned to control his thoughts, if he'd tried to tell his friends what was happening, he'd still be alive today."

"That was sad Louis."

"Well it was a sad way to go wasn't it. The fool."

"True."

Myself and Louis paid tribute by standing in silence saluting him. It was a strange few moments, realising that Crimson would now be just a memory. The only plus side was that we'd get the Rodent Key. He'd been so reluctant to part with it before.

I stood there gazing at my nibbled friend and started to daydream. I had always liked that arrogant half-breed and I will miss him. He was to me like cream is to milk. Louis always described him as being a bit sour but I reckon he was top. He was as rich and creamy as day one. But now he's going to become just another of the fallen in this war against hamster control. Oh how I would have liked to have known him for longer. My sister Rachel used to talk of a hero she knew called Crimson when she was young. She always gave a radiant smile when his name cropped up. I'll never forget her tearful eyes when he'd disappear one fine morning. Sadness was written across her face and she became distant. She was crying the day he left, apparently he was going back to France. It's odd that it was probably the same Crimson, I guess there can't be too many Crimson Pigs' in the world, after all. She told us he'd given her his favourite Crimson smile when he went. He also gave her a Crimson hankie. He'd written across the torn silk the letters DM DM. I thought it a very bizarre action for ones' friend to give them a second hand hankie with writing on, oh how blind I was. I really didn't understand the full meaning. I remember once I cleaned some spilled milk with it when I noticed it hanging out of her left pocket. No wonder she had gone berserk, that she had slandered my name across the whole street in front of all my family and friends. She hated it when I mocked the letters on it. I always used to say they stood for *Dumb Mouse, Dumb Mouse*. She told me it meant nothing of the sort. She said that one day, when I grew up she'd tell me. I guess I never did. The Ssssylfia spoke of DM DM meaning, of course, Dark Matter Does Matter- I guess I understand now, but it's too late isn't it…

"Jane! Jane, snap out of it!"

"Oh sorry Louis I was just reminiscing about my sister, sorry. Hang on….Look!"

Above our heads the tortoiseshell scratcher was scurrying around inside the faith safe. Suddenly two bottles came into view.

The bottles flew through the air. The scratcher's tail had knocked them and they came hurtling towards us, faster and faster. One shattered on a book that was sticking out and the magical juice inside spurted out all over me, I was soaking.

"Urrr!" I screamed. The other bottle lay broken on the floor by the half-eaten Crimson. It was a nasty sight to see him in such a mangled state...

I was desperately upset. I stood there for a few moments looking all around but my sense of hearing, for a split second, had gone. A picture on the wall caught my attention. I saw a blackboard with a funny, familiar shape drawn on it. I was thinking, where have I seen this before? I also saw, on the shelves, jars of tablets, some saying MIN, others saying MAX.... and then I remembered! In Andrew's kitchen, at the end-of-the-tracks in Mor's Den. He too had these funny tablet jars and he too had this funny shape in a picture frame on his wall. I wondered what it meant...

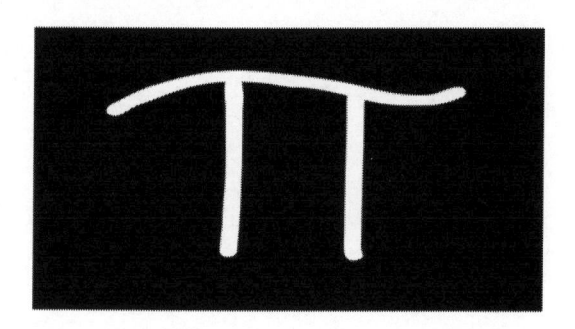

"Jane," shouted Louis, "go through that door, I saw some towels to clean yourself up with on the left-hand side when we came in."

I struggled through the door Louis was on about and was even more stunned. Looking one way I could see Louis in the library, skulking behind a chair leg and trying to avoid the hungry scratcher. But when I looked the other way I could see no towels at all. I saw lots of unpredictables, scurrying around; I was back at the WaterLoo station! How odd. I remember rubbing my eyes and pinching myself, but no matter what I did, it was true. If I told Louis, would it be true then? I wondered whether, if Louis were to come scampering along to join me only to discover that I had been telling porky pies, he would ever speak to me again? I guessed it was a risk I'd have to take. Whether it was the right time for such a risk is something that only the Sacred Scrolls would know. It is written that if you can pitch and toss and win or lose but never disclose your loss, then you'll be a proper mouse, my friend. I hope I can pitch and toss and win but well, here goes… I ran for the opening and shouted towards my only remaining colleague, "Louis, over here Louis!"

"What? What is it? Can't you see I'm trying my hardest not to be seen. It's not a game this you know. If that scratcher sees me I'm as dead as Crimson, then you'd be in it. You'd have to save all the stray mice on your own. Do you think you could do it Jane? Well do you?" he whispered.

"Look Louis, how about treating me with a little respect. I've come this far with you, the least you could do is treat me as an equal."

"This is the wrong time for an argument; don't you think you should wipe that juice off your clothes? Good grief… your pockets are starting to swell!"

I looked down at my waist and what Louis had said was true. The juice must have seeped into my pockets and reacted with the Professor and Jim in their shells, although the Professor seemed to be swelling at a faster rate. I plucked him from my pocket first and out of the corner of my eye I saw Louis hurtling towards me. I was terrified. It is written that the sensation of fear causes heart attacks if accompanied by too much stress. I realised that I must try to keep calm. Stay focused. Then, with a little bit of luck I should be alive to see the rest of the day…

DONK!

Louis flew right into me and knocked me over. Imagine an enormous monster charging you from thirty paces, it was like that. I don't mean that Louis' fat, he's just larger than me. He's well built. He's the kind of mouse that displays outer strength to go along nicely with his inner strength. I guess he's a kind of athlete. A decathlon-type. The sort of mouse who could compete in all types of events. So I shouldn't really blame him for knocking me down then, I think, or should I?

"Jane!" Louis shouted. He was lying on top of me at the time. "Why didn't you move out of the way when you saw me coming?"

"I dunno?"

"Err, never mind." Louis started staring at the Professor (he was still stuck inside the pecan shell and lying on the floor in front of us). I plucked the pecan containing Jim out of my pocket too, but he was motionless. I noticed that Louis had the Rodent Key wrapped around his neck as well as Crimson's locket, and the crimson coloured hat and scarf. I guess he was being his usual self. He had done the necessary and got the key to trade with the hamsters but for sentimental reasons he'd got Crimson's locket and clothes.

"Look at the Professor, he's changing." I squeaked.

First of all we saw a darkened pecan lying on the steps. It was about three times its normal size. There was a large crack running down the left-hand side of it. We then noticed a tiny paw trying to force its way out. It was like watching an egg hatch. Yes! That's what it was like. It was like watching life begin. Bits of the shell started to break free. It was like the juice had made the shell crumble into flaky pieces.

POP! It went.

And out popped the Professor. He was holding his head in a funny way, but apart from that he looked fine. Louis stuffed the key and Crimson's locket, hat and scarf into the inventions sack and breathed a sigh of relief. Next our attention swung to Jim. He was only about twice the size of a normal pecan, why was this? Why was he only half done? A crack started to form down the right hand side of his shell, just like the Professor's. But it looked as though Jim didn't have the strength to just pop out. We could see a tiny paw but try as he might he was stuck fast...

Suddenly Louis noticed we were back on the steps at WaterLoo. "Jane! Look where we are."

"I know. It's odd isn't it?"

"What's been going on?" asked the weary Professor. "All I remember was drinking some juice in that chalky place? Wait, we've gotta find Crimson Pigs, that's it."

"He's dead," I said sadly.

"Sorry Jane, what was that?"

"He's dead Professor. He died trying to help us, to help you," cried Louis. He then opened the sack of inventions and showed the Professor his locket, the Rodent Key and some of Crimson's clothes.

"What? Dead? But how?"

"Yes, he's dead," said Louis.

"Yeah, and he died in such an awful way," I muttered.

"Dead you say, but when? Are you sure?"

"A hungry scratcher got him through that door way....." Louis pointed to the door. It sort of shimmered in front of us, then it seemed to wink at us as it vanished.

"Did you see that?" asked the Professor.

"Yeah," myself and Louis mumbled together.

"But why is Jim still a pecan? I don't understand?"

"I think, Professor, because he only half believes in the Sacred Scrolls. That's why he's only half your size. Your shell was massive. He's probably in pain in there......wait, did you hear that?"

"Get...me....out...of here?" squeaked the pecan.

"It's Jim!" I yelled. Louis grabbed hold of him to help force the shell open but it was no good.

"Look, let me have a go too..."

"And me..." we all pulled and tugged at Jim. I saw one of his whiskers poking out of a slit and grabbed that. I was pulling and pulling until....

TWANG!

"Owwww! Stop....it!" Jim was howling. He was in immense pain.

"Look, it's no good. Professor have you got anything in there that might help?" Louis pointed to his sack.

"Err, let me try this.....It's called a Max-Crowbar. I invented it because I thought that if I ever got stuck inside something I'd need it. But it should do the trick on that pecan." Sure enough, the Professor pushed the hooked end into the slit in the shell, and we all grabbed the other end.

"Right on three we'll all yank together. Here we go, one...two...threeee!!"

CRUNCH!

"Yes! It's working." I squeaked. The Max-Crowbar prised the lid off the top of the pecan and Jim was free. He staggered out. Louis went straight to him to check that he was okay. It was wonderful to have him back. Well, it was wonderful to have both of my brothers back with me. I say brothers but we were comrades, as not related by blood. I guess Paul was a non related brother to Max and he always described him as his stepbrother... Oh no! Wait! I suddenly had a terrible thought. Crimson had Paul, so maybe Paul had been eaten too.

"I got the hazelnut," smiled Louis.

"What a relief," said Max and me together.

Louis showed it to us and stuffed it deep into his pocket once more, "I'll hold onto it for a while, if it is Paul that is..."

6. Jim's Rat-Route Revelation

Jim was standing for the first time in ages. We were perched on the edge of the steps at the front entrance of WaterLoo station. It was funny that neither Jim nor the Professor had met Crazy, or got to know Crimson. Yes, they both knew he had an attitude, but they didn't know that his lack of teamwork would lead to his eventual demise. If only he'd told us he was heading for that faith safe, then we could've helped him. We could've distracted that scratcher and maybe he would still be alive today.

Jim was in a funny mood. He said that the magical juices had an odd taste but that they'd also changed his appearance somewhat. It was all very odd as the Professor hadn't changed at all.

"Are you all right old chap?" asked Louis.

"Urrr, agony, agony,...." Jim replied.

"Good," said Louis. "I think we should sleep here tonight and see what happens tomorrow. Is that okay with you Max?"

"What, err, what did we miss except Crimson's death? Anything interesting? Anything you want to tell me?"

"Well Max, I mean Professor, normally I'd say no. But the lesson I've learnt from the past two days tells me it is better to inform your friends what's going on just in case you end up with egg on your face."

"What egg? Was it from the round face?" I asked. I admit I was tired but I didn't understand Louis sometimes.

"I didn't mean to be pretentious. It is written that truth outweighs its worth in gold fourteen times over."

"Does it really say that Louis?" asked a worn out Jim.

"No! Ha! Ha! You see Jim, I can tell white lies too, but the difference between mine and yours is now we're safe. Do you get it?"

"Yeah, like a house on fire," he giggled.

"What house Jim?" I asked. They'd lost me. I was confused again.

"Don't worry about it," replied Jim, he climbed back inside part of the shell and then dozed off. Louis pulled him by his ears to a safe section on the higher level and we relaxed.

There were quite a few unpredictables around, but Louis managed to secure a warm spot for our evening nap. Jim looked cute lying on the ground. But as time tottered on I could see Louis was worried about Paul and Richard and the possibility that they were both connected in the same way. He sat there with the hazelnut on his lap; he sniffed it and listened to it but it confused him. Would Paul really be inside this nut? Why did Andrew specifically choose a hazelnut rather than a pecan for this rodent? How did Crimson manage to find it at Chalky Farm amongst all those other nuts? Or did he find it elsewhere? We don't know the real facts as he didn't tell us.

It's true Louis had rescued the Rodent Key, but would that be enough? I watched as he took Crimson's locket out of the inventions sack and shook it. It made a splashing sound. It no longer had RedBush's tea leaves in it as Crimson had tipped them out at Chalky Farm. I wondered if Dark Matter liquid was now inside it! Yes, it must be magical juice. Louis must have really risked his life to get that liquid. It must have been from that leaking bottle on the floor of the library.

"Louis! Louis! Is that magical juice?"

"Yeah."

"How did you...?"

"Don't ask..."

"Oh come on, tell me, please?"

"I prised the claws of the tortoiseshell scratcher with a piece of bottle. I was trying to grab the locket, anyway the bottle was already shattered on the floor so I scooped some up with the locket. Then I escaped! That's why I hit you with such immense force. I was running for my life."

Louis led the way to the higher level again. Where would our next mission take us? I looked at my friends and felt happy, but then a cold shiver ran up and down my spine and my hairs stood on end. At this higher level there was another picture on the wall. That shape had appeared again, the one from Andrew's Den and from the library. I looked at Max and he saw it too. So I asked him what it meant.

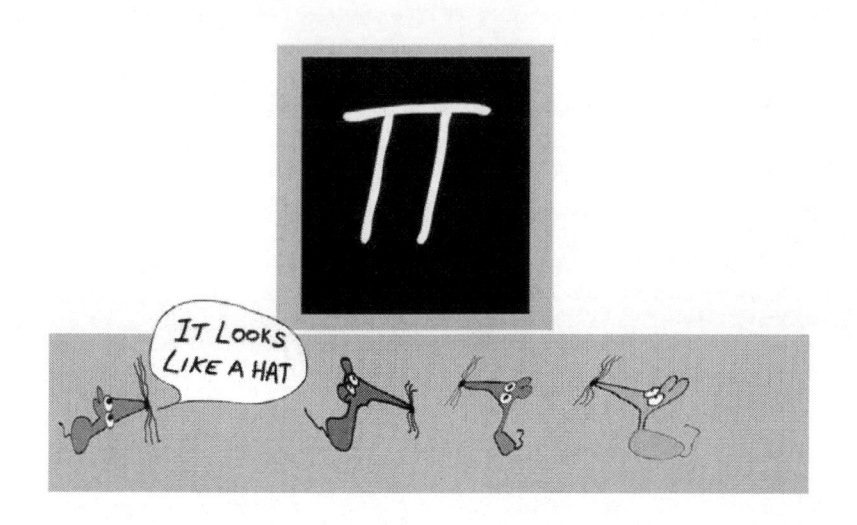

"What does that symbol mean," I asked and pointed to it.

"It is a symbol used in mathematics," he replied.

"But what does it mean?" asked Jim.

"It's known as Pi- not the type you can eat but the type that can be used in mathematical explanations. I believe it can be used in travel."

"I think it looks more like a hat," said Jim.

"It's not a hat," moaned Louis.

"It's Pi, I told you that!" groaned the Professor.

"Well it doesn't look very tasty, does it? There's no base, no crust; I think you're mistaken," quipped Jim.

"There are two types of Pi- if you listened to Max just then you would've heard him say that," moaned Louis.

"What? Like a pecan pie and a chicken pie, you mean?"

"No!"

"Well, if it's not about food then I'm not interested." And with that Jim settled down to sleep. But then suddenly he shouted, "It's about the Rat-Routes then!"

"What?" we all said together.

"Every time we go through a Rat-Route the date shifts four years."

"What?" we all said again.

"Pi and travel are connected. So Rat-Routes are connected too, yes?"

"I don't know what you mean?" I answered.

"Look if I can't eat it then it's about travel, that's what Max said, so if it's about travel it must be about the weird methodology of Rat-Routes. I believe it is written that one weird thing deserves another."

"You made that one up!" growled Louis.

"Then maybe it should!" moaned Jim. He winked at me, giggled and settled down to sleep again.

"Is, err....oh look....." I pointed to the blackness, it began to light up, as though a mechanical beast was coming any second. Suddenly, almost like clockwork it arrived and the Ssssylfia hovered in front of us once more.

> WIPE THE SMOKE
> FROM HIS EYES
> TO DISCOVER THE
> WONDROUS SURPRIZE

Suddenly Jim leaped to his feet. He turned towards Louis and smiled. He waved at me, and winked at the Professor. We all knew what he was gonna say because we all thought the same now, we'd become a united team. I wondered if we would ever be discovered by the rodents of the future. I guess that'll only happen if we become the pace setters. We all watched as Jim stretched out his arms and shouted, "Here we go again…"

**Fitness is a factor,
for those that struggle will get caught,
and creating a new White Energy will be their fault**

1. Déjà vu

So Crimson had died and us four friends were back together on our mission to save Richard, the 2nd in line to the throne of Jerboa. Originally we just wanted to be free from our sawdust prison, but now we had new goals. We had a mission and this was to help all the rodents of this world. The Dark Energy search is I think, just a smoke screen concealing what we really want, or need to find. Why find something that no one can see? Who cares really? Yes, we were still learning, I admit that. Crimson had taught me and Louis so much. Jim and the Professor missed out on his knowledge due to their own silliness. Crazy the rat had tried to teach us new worrying facts too. He had put doubts in our heads as to the validity of the Sacred Scrolls and the reasons why Jerbil MacTaggart, the legend that all rodents look up to, was just a sham. Crazy spoke of Jim being the inaugural cog in the motion of our lives. But Jim doesn't know this yet. Should I tell him? Would he laugh at me? But Louis was still convinced that he was the chosen ONE, not Jim. And yes, Louis had been a good leader to us and to Jim, but maybe the tide was turning in Jim's favour. Crimson had taken on the mantle of power, but his lack of communication proved his downfall. Would Jim's lack of communication end his life too?

Dark Matter, the substance inside the bottles that we had found near WaterLoo, is a potion that changes various things into other things. That 'hat-type' symbol that I had seen in the library that belonged to the whiskered unpredictable, and again at the higher level at WaterLoo station, may well be very relevant. Andrew Archdeacon, the crazy chef from Mor's Den also idolised this symbol. The Professor had theories too, unproven as to their meaning.

We sat there for a few minutes on the higher level listening to Louis chant away as usual. It was nice to be together again as a group. I had missed that.

The Ssssylfia had emerged a second time from the blackness with an even more bizarre message, but the funny thing was that Louis said he'd seen it before, in High Gate…

> **FARADAY**
> **OR**
> **FARAWAY**
> **WHEN ELECTRICITY**
> **& MAGNETISM**
> **JOIN AS ONE**

"I recognised that riddle," said Louis.

"From where?" asked a puzzled Professor.

"From High Gate. It was on a tombstone in the cemetery."

"Is that before or after I was captured by those scratchers?"

"After."

"But you never mentioned any of this before and that was ages ago," I moaned.

"It's only now that it has become relevant. What's the point in me saying it before without a reason," replied Louis. We sat there with our paws dangling over the edge and looking at the tracks beneath us. "Crimson may have known what it meant, maybe I should have told him."

"Too late now," squeaked Jim.

"I know, and I regret it."

"I still can't believe he's dead," I muttered, "but you kept his things, why?"

"He did not wear his crimson scarf always, and he did not wear his coat, at all. This hat and scarf that are in the sack of inventions he would've wanted buried with him when he died," sighed Louis.

"Is it true Crimson's a goner?" asked Jim. He looked upset as he didn't realise how much of a fool Crimson really was.

"Yes Jim. I rescued his locket, hat and scarf. As he scrapped with that tortoiseshell scratcher his hat and scarf flew off but his coat got tangled in the scratchers claws. Anyway, I left his coat, grabbed the locket, hazelnut, hat and scarf; it was a tense few minutes. Actually, look, I'll wear them in his honour."

He put them on, although they were a bit of a loose fit, Crimson having been a larger proportioned rodent.

"Yeah, I guess they suit you in a funny sort of way" I smiled.

"Take them off, where's your respect?" moaned the Professor.

"Okay, I'll put them back in the sack as we may yet find them useful."

"So, after our sleep where are we off to?" enquired Jim, "we don't know of this king's church place that the hamsters speak off. What do you suggest?"

"I suggest we go back to place of the hamster's origins in Kennington. For only through the wise old hamster can we understand the logic and the minds of the newcomers in this deed we seek."

"Louis, did you understand the Ssssylfia riddle about wiping smoke away?" asked Jim. "I reckon it was talking about itself, after all it is smoke. Maybe we'll find out who or what controls it, surely there must be a scientific explanation, nothing should be as complicated as all that, should it?"

"I dunno. I do however know that the Ssssylfia is a manifestation, a vision, a helping paw in our search for Dark Energy. It's not smoke."

"Well, you're a fine help."

"Well, I try. Ha! Ha!"

"So it's off to Kennington for us then. Oh well, so be it...." sighed Jim again. He was fiddling with dirt that must have come out of the pecan shell and smeared it onto his furry body. But the more he twiddled with it, the more grubby he became and this made him angry. I watched as he picked at a large clotted lump of muck that had attached itself to his right paw. But this lump then became glued somehow to his longest whisker. He pulled it and twisted it; he made squeaky, groaning noises; he most definitely was not a happy little mouse…

2. Jim's Injury

We all set off for Ken's adopted home town. On a moving sign, way above our heads on the higher level, written in the unpredictable's language, was the direction these mechanical beasts were going. Sometimes it read that they were going to the end-of-the-tracks, to Mor's Den; yet at other times it said Kennington. I guess it was obvious really that the hamsters controlled the flow of the mechanical beasts. Hamsters were known to do that. They were an organisation. A gangster formation. A mafia-type rodent. Control was, after all, in the blood that churned within their twisted brains. Louis reckoned it was because of them that bizarre happenings occurred in the tunnels. Sometimes we could hear over the intercom that the beast would be terminating at Kennington, that it wouldn't be reaching the end-of-the-tracks.

"Why does the mechanical beast terminate at Kennington Louis? Is there a large influx of hamster activity?" asked Jim, "because that's what Jane reckons."

"It's rather a complicated story but here goes," answered Louis, but Jim began to shuffle around to get comfy. He eventually climbed on to one of the metal seats. "Jim keep still! It all started to go haywire when that Scottish unpredictable arrived with her hamsters. She...."

Alas Jim fell off his metal seat and he slipped through the bars onto the higher level. He landed at an awkward angle on the concrete floor and this caused him to yell out, "Ow! Oh my leg is killing me?"

"Jim! Shhhh! I'm talking!" snapped Louis.

"But my leg hurts. I think I've broken it." We went over to him and he looked in immense pain. Louis started poking and tweaking him on the injured leg.

"Ow! Stop it!"

"Stop complaining I'm trying to understand the problem."

"Ow! That hurts! Ow!"

"Stop whinging!"

"Well stop poking me! Ow!"

"We're gonna have to get him to a doctor. An unpredictable with whiskers known as a vet."

"Why are they called vets?" asked Jim. He pepped up a bit after thinking of a ghastly unpredictable touching him.

"Jim, they're called vets for two reasons. Vet is a short word for veterinary surgeon, you know the ONE that makes you live or die. I guess in a way he's like our creator."

"So what's the other kind of vet then?"

"That's would be a veteran. Like an old and wise rodent and as we are seeking the knowledge from a hamster I reckon that we may as well get him to cure you too. If you can be cured!"

"What do you mean, if?"

"Well, if you're beyond repair you'll live your days lying on a bed of strawberries being fed for the rest of your life."

"Sounds great, I've dreamt of that. When am I going?"

"I know you have, we all saw that dream too. Look, we must find this veteran hamster I think. I'm not sure an unpredictable would be as helpful. And before any of you say it," he looked deep into our eyes and thoughts, (as we all thought 'what hamster would help a mouse?') "this hamster will help any injured rodent. It is written that MacDrid is an ally to all rodent kind. We're going now, look team, I've got Jim." Louis hoisted him over his shoulder and pointed to a mechanical beast, "let's get that beast over there, okay."

He pointed to a really knackered looking one. It looked like it had been around for 100 years. "I guess this is a vet of the mechanical beasts," joked the Professor.

"Yeah," laughed Louis. We all clambered on. Louis tied a piece of pecan shell around Jim's left leg, he said it would act as a temporary brace. He tied it up with Jim's longest whisker which wasn't at all to Jim's liking.

"Do you realise how long it's taken me to get that whisker that size. It's by far the best whisker of any of us. It's gonna get ruined." He sulked on the edge of the bumper. The beast then started making clunking noises. It started shaking and stuttering like a vet mouse. The unpredictables inside were becoming impatient, well, all except one. She was a young blonde haired type. Obviously she was a safe one as she had no earrings. She just sat there dreaming away, watching the scruffy ear-ringed youth cursing and shouting at the grey whiskered guard. After a couple more attempts to move we were off. Sparks were continually flying as we headed into the blackness. Louis said that next time we'd be better off going on a cleaner, newer one.

"It is written that cleanliness is next to happiness," sighed Jim. "A clean, perfectly groomed mouse looks down on the scruffs. Oh the shame! Oh how will I ever be able to hold my head up again in public? I'll just be like the rest of you fools. I'll scamper along the road looking dirty, looking unwashed, looking like a vagrant."

"You're always slamming us as untidy mice. I realise that you've set your own standards, but if you could only see that if you could curb your selfish side you'd be king of the castle," moaned Louis.

"Which castle's that Louis?" I asked.

"Well, after we've seen this vet hamster I think we should head for the town that lacks a king. It's called Elephant Castle."

"I don't wanna become king in a place where big cumbersome creatures roam freely. In fact I've heard of that place, isn't that faraway or Faraday or something? Isn't that where a large grey elephant stands by the side of concrete heaven?"

"I'm impressed that you've been reading Jim."

"Well, there was nothing else to do whilst stuck inside that shell. Actually it is written that at this elephant's town there is a concrete island that houses the silver cube. What's this silver cube Louis?"

"I dunno?"

"I think we need to go there, maybe it's near the king's church. After all you said it had a king. Yes, we'll see the vet hamster, find out where these reservoir hamsters want there meeting and if it's close by, head for the silver cube where the elephants live and then find the Dark Energy."

"I don't think we're ready for the Dark Energy yet."

"Why Louis? Is it because Dark Energy is that wall at Bell-Sized Park after all? Is it that you are starting to believe me when I say I've seen it? Was it not a wall in that vision that portrayed you as a slimy Alligator? I really think that we don't need to look anywhere else as it's in Bell-Sized Park unless that spider has eaten it," chirped Jim.

"Spiders don't eat walls! Anyway, I'm gonna ignore you for a bit, this is getting silly. Now, Crimson spoke of different worlds. Lots of different countries. And he said we can't even think of this Dark Energy until we know about everything else."

"But what does he know? He said the Professor's inventions were his didn't he?" moaned Jim.

"Yeah, good point." Louis sneaked over to where the Professor was sleeping and grabbed the sack off him. Unfortunately this woke him up. You see, the Professor had tied one of his whiskers around the cord that closes the sack up. When Louis pulled the sack it triggered pain inside the Professor's face. Thus causing him to jump to his feet....

"Argh! What's happening? What's going on?" Louis continued pulling and pulling and then the Professor's whisker finally gave way, it twanged and broke in two.

"Got them!" screamed Louis.

"Louis, give them back they're mine."

"No they're not."

"Yes they are," squeaked the Professor.

"No!"

"Why?"

"Because Crimson spoke of them being his, that's why."

"So you believe him over me. Me who has saved your bacon so many times. Me who was with you from the start in Clapham. Me, that won the court battle. Ah, ha! It is written that you can't try a mouse for the same case twice, so give them back."

"No!"

"Jane, please tell him that he's being way out of order,....please...."

"You are in the wrong Louis!"

Louis looked me in the eyes as if to say I was making a grave mistake. Then he threw the sack at the Professor shouting and cursing at him in the process. "Go on then, take them. I can't believe... oh well... it's just... nothing.." He walked right to the furthest edge of the bumper where Jim comforted him a little. He wiped the sweat from his fluffy brow. Jim was one of those characters who would sometimes act normal, almost to the point of caring. Unfortunately the clunky beast we were on stopped in the blackness. Its lights went out and there were no tunnel lights. Everything was even darker than normal...

3. On Route to Kennington

Usually it is pitch black in the tunnels but as the beast drives through them it sparks on the tracks causing flashes of light and strobe-effect images. But now, as we were not moving we couldn't see anything.

"What's happening?" Jim shrieked.

"Shhh! The beast will come back to life soon." Louis was trying to keep us all patient. I'd never experienced total darkness before, it was scary, but after about two minutes our eyes started adjusting to the blackness, for there were tiny slithers of light piercing the darkness and mottling the walls. I'd never noticed these before. Then I saw what looked like two cabbages flying through the air! Were these two rats that were part of that Sprout army, or was this another silly daydream?

"Can you see inside the carriage?" asked a voice, "I can just about make out the unpredictables. Look at them. They're just sitting there with blank expressions. They look like lost sheep. Ha! Ha!"

I think it was Jim that was speaking. Actually it must have been Jim, no one else says useless annoying things like him.

"Shhhh! Jim. The unpredictables are like us now, don't mock them. It is written that unpredictables are peace loving creatures at night."

"Louis are you telling me that you've never been chased by an outraged unpredictable at night time?"

"Yes."

"Well then I guess that's why you're blind to the truth. Is it not also written that blind mice can be blind in different ways," moaned Jim.

"I don't remember that one."

"Then maybe, just maybe you'd understand the logic of truth." Jim slammed Louis in the face with his right paw like an uppercut. Louis retaliated with a kick to the ribs. That started a mass scrap. They would take no prisoners. The Professor joined in only to be bashed on the chin. It was awful.

It reminded me of the kind of fight I used to witness with my seven sisters. We used to play merrily everyday, then on Friday afternoons at about 3.30pm we used to watch some unpredictables fighting. They tended to fight for silly things like one of them would grab the other one's cap and this would provoke a flare up. Firstly they'd try to negotiate a deal, or should I say the one who'd stolen the cap would. It would be like, if you want the cap back you've got to do all the other one's homework for a week in their writing style. Well, the other unpredictable didn't agree the terms and therefore, at the allocated time, they both met by the mill for a battle of fists.

Sad that Jim and Louis have adopted the same ragging sprees as twisted young unpredictables. Of course these unpredictables wore earrings. It was too obvious to mention really but well, I did anyway.

"Have you had enough?" Louis stood over a bruised Jim. He started whinging about the only reason why Louis beat him was that he was injured before they started. Which of course was true. Louis then offered Jim the paw of friendship.

"I don't want your help! I want to be far away from the likes of you!"

"Suit yourself." That was it for Louis. Suddenly the lights flickered and sparked back on. The mechanical beast came back to life and we headed for Kennington again.

"Come on then guys, get up!" shouted Louis.

We all stood and watched as the beast pulled into the new higher level, its termination point. Louis ordered us off before the grey whiskered unpredictable guard came round and chased us off. Louis was still shouting and still rude to Jim. He didn't like him at all. I guess it was the same kind of relationship that Louis had with Crimson. After he stole Crimson's clothes he did display pig-like characteristics.

"Which way then?" asked a struggling Jim.

"This way." Louis pointed to a vast flight of stairs. The escalator was, for some reason, not working. We struggled up the steps but Jim was trailing badly, his supposedly fractured leg was really slowing us down and Louis didn't want to help him. So it was left to myself and the Professor to give him a helping paw. When we came out of the station Louis said we should head for the park. We wandered lonely as a cloud, travelling down one of the concrete rivers. It felt like a journey into the unknown. It was funny that feeling. Which ever new place we went to felt scary but also every new place was the unknown, literally. This never ending expedition into uncharted country; did this sum up my life? Jim was getting really tired and the further we walked the more argumentative he got. When we came around a large corner building we got soaked by muddy water, Louis had rushed out ahead of us and was waiting for us to fall into his dirty trap. We were absolutely filthy.

"Look at the state of us?" cried Jim.

"Ha! Ha! Got ya," giggled Louis. Yet he was the only one smiling, the swine!

"Louis, my whiskers are just so dirty it's...it's...oh never mind," said Jim as he sulked whilst hobbling along.

"Well Louis, why did you do that?" I moaned.

"Yeah why?" complained the Professor.

"It was just an impulse thing okay."

"No! No, it's not okay...." That was it, both myself and the Professor refused to speak to him.

Then Jim came out with a vindictive rant at our leader; I had wanted to say something like this but Jim got there first. "It is written that if you annoy your friends too much they'll send you to Coventry. Well, I don't know where that is but if ever I do I'll be thinking of this day."

We all stopped by the side of another big puddle in an attempt to clean our faces. I'd never been so dirty in all my life. I couldn't believe Louis had done that. Normally he was so well mannered. I guess the scroll that tells us 'when the clock strikes twelve one of your team will act like a pumpkin' was true. Louis was most definitely our pumpkin today.

"I'm gonna call you pumpkin face for that!" I blasted.

"Why?" quizzed Louis.

"Because pumpkins are useless, fat vegetables that are only used once a year."

"But I don't understand?"

"Well, pumpkin face, I don't care."

"Yeah Jane that's funny. Hey pumpkin face, how are you pumpkin face? Can you look me in the face, pumpkin face?" Jim joked.

And that was that. We were four mice struggling and soaking (well, except Louis) through a park in a land famous for hamsters. Could it get any worse?

4. Grabbed

A couple of minutes passed and we all sat on the grass. The Professor was so unhappy he didn't even fancy a run. Louis had ruined our tempo and moods. As we sat there we saw a dark cloud descending on us. We all looked into the air and could see some horrid dark winged creatures. They were crows scribbling in the sky and circling overhead and looking extremely hungry.

We all just ran and ran and ran. Louis said we should head for the large building thing in the centre of the park. After about thirty seconds of intense scampering we reached it. Louis forced the door open and we scurried in. I say we, but Jim was lagging behind. We clambered onto a window-ledge and could see him miles back, hobbling across the park. One of the dark creatures swooped down from the heavens and hoisted him up and away. It was like watching the hunter get its prey. It was awful. Just because he couldn't run as fast as us meant that he got caught.

"Look that creature has got him," shouted the Professor.

"I think these dark creatures are the crows that liaise with the hamsters of this town."

"I've heard of them too, I think," I squeaked. "Isn't that the place where that elephant lives too, although I've never seen an elephant in a nest?"

"Maybe, but if we can somehow mock these crows then we can trick them. It is written that crows likes berries. If we can tempt the crows into a bush of berries we can capture their minds and save Jim," squeaked Louis. He was crouched very low and was peeking at Jim through the slits of his fingers.

"It is written that a crow in the paw is worth two in the bush, therefore I reckon if we can get two crows we've got a slim chance of helping Jim?" stuttered the Professor.

"Yeah, look...." Louis pointed to a bush with lush, rich berries. "If we go over there and start eating the berries we'll be teasing them. They'll drop Jim for the greed of food."

"I've got these inventions here, they're called Max-Reins. If we toss them over the heads of these creatures we can fly on them too! The creatures will no doubt panic and lead us straight to their nest."

"Good idea Professor. After three, then we charge the bushes; ready, one.. two.. threeee!!!"

Unfortunately though, the crow holding Jim was disappearing over the horizon. Would we ever see our chubby friend again?

We all scampered together. The Professor was slightly slower because he was carrying all of Crimson's extras. There seemed to be quite a lot of bumps and loose twigs which were making it a little tricky to run. I fell twice and Louis fell once, but luck was on our side as we made it quite quickly to the bushes.

"Now we have to rattle the crows. Come on!" yelled Louis. He said if we ate a couple of berries they'd get jealous and attack.

"Look up there Louis!" I squeaked.

"It is written that when the night is drawing in and the a the Sun begins to set, its White Energy turns to Red Energy."

"I think you're right.. look! The sky is turning red!" I squealed. It was just as the Sacred Scroll predicted, yet if this scroll was true then the rats' belief that they were fakes was maybe, just maybe, wrong. And if they were wrong about the scrolls maybe they would be wrong about the fake Jerbil MacTaggart legend.

Way above our heads three crows swooped down to attack us. One each, that's how the Professor put it. As soon as the first one got close to me the Professor slung his Max-Reins over the creature's head. Then another one came down and he did the same. Myself and Louis then boarded our feathered slaves. We watched as the Professor captured the final creature. Louis reckoned that if we kicked them in their plumage they'd react in such a way that they'd be desperate to get home.

"Well I'm a definitely kicking then," screeched the Professor.

We watched as he was hoisted into the air. Alas the Max-Reins on his crow weren't fixed tightly enough and they slipped, leaving the Professor dangling, upside down, beneath the flying creature. It must have been a bizarre sight to the drunk and shabby looking unpredictables who lived in the park. Next, Louis kicked his crow. He too swung upside down as the Max-Reins slipped and when I kicked my crow I too was left hanging upside down from the feathered beast. It was a horrid feeling, really scary...

I'd never really liked heights. In fact upside down on a creature that zooms through the sky is my kind of hell. If ever I grow old, I'll never forget that day. I'll remember that it's good to keep fit so that I'm not the slowest around and if a nasty unpredictable or scratcher tries to grab me it'll be easier to run away....

"Louis! Louis! Can you hear me?" I shouted. All I could see was the back of his head. He wasn't holding onto the Max-Reins like me. He was trying desperately to keep hold of the locket so that none of the magical liquid would spill. I shouted again, "Louis! Louis! Where are we going?"

I heard a faint murmur, he said, "How would I know?"

"Louis! Louis! Look down there," said the Professor. I couldn't see at all because I was behind him too, so I had no idea where he was pointing. "Do you see that silver cube Louis?"

"Just about...What about it?"

"I can't see! I can't see!" I screamed.

" Louis! Is that the one you spoke of earlier?"

"It might be, yes. I've never actually seen it though, especially upside down at sixty feet in the air. Max! Please can you stop talking to me, I'm trying to....Oh no, we're coming down...."

Firstly I heard the Professor's crow land, it came down using the body of my friend as a cushion to break its fall. Max rolled along like a ball. It was quite similar to what had happened before, at Arch Way, but much worse. My crow turned and at last I could see what was happening. I watched as Louis' crow came down in a bizarre manner. This one swooped down. I guess he kind of free fell and it must have scared Louis half to death. My crow was older and managed to tilt its wings and glide down quite elegantly. We all staggered away from our crows, but the weird thing was, they didn't attack. They were quite dumb. They hadn't noticed that we'd hitched lifts at all. Then I saw that their eyes were swirling. Had they been brainwashed? If it was that easy to control these dark creatures was it possible that we too would be controlled?

"That was a hideous descent," muttered Louis. He had blood shot eyes and seemed to be trembling. Panic was written all over his face. The Professor was slightly bruised but I was relatively unscathed. Louis then pointed towards the silver cube, outside of which stood a large crow. The area around the cube had four statues of elephants; it was a strange place.

"This is what Jim was going on about. He always wondered what it was and now we'll find out," sighed Louis.

"So what is it Louis?"

"The silver cube must be related to the Ssssylfia vision. Faraway or Faraday or something. Let me think for a minute and try to remember what I saw."

"Jane, I saw the Ssssylfia vision on a tombstone in High Gate and wondered if it was the ONE. Faraday is the home of the vet hamster, the wise one. Maybe this hamster is the ONE we seek. I believe this place is the home of MacDrid."

"Louis, do you know there's a crow guarding the main entrance. What do we do now?" I asked.

"Leave it to me." He walked over towards it. It looked like he was trying to drum up some kind of deal but after about five minutes he came scampering back.

"What's happening?" asked the Professor.

"Well it seems only hamsters, crows and female rodents are allowed to enter the sacred silver chamber."

"So what are you saying?" I was petrified. "Do you want me to go in and rescue Jim on my own, is that it? Well I don't think I'm skilled enough and I'm too scared."

"Well actually I've got a different plan. Professor you'll have to dress in Crimson's clothes, his hat, scarf and locket okay? That way you'll look like RedBush, the Collective member that Crimson impersonated. Hopefully they won't query why you are so small. And Jane, you'll be okay because you're female anyway."

"But what about you Louis, what are you to do?" questioned the Professor. He looked equally as worried as me. I guess that when the weight of danger and responsibility fell upon us, we were both guilty of being chickens.

"I'm going to revert back to the way I was brought up. I'll tell you this Professor because you missed it. I'm, err...well, err.. I used to be called Louise." Louis hesitated as he spoke and started rubbing his eyes; the Professor slightly stunned. "You see where I was brought up there were no male mice. My family smuggled me in. It made me see things in a new light, gave me a new focus if you like. I can think like a male or female mouse and there is a big difference you know."

"All right, say you become Louise, will you change your style and mannerisms?"

"Only slightly. I shall comb my whiskers. I shall prune my eye brows. I shall walk in beauty like the night and scamper in the same manner as Jane, as if we came from the same flickering flame."

The Professor was a little shocked by Louis' outburst. Still it didn't affect his judgement of him which I found impressive. Jim had been so outraged before but the Professor wasn't. I guess this proved that he was much more mature than Jim.

"So, when are we going in?" he asked Louis.

"Just give me a couple of minutes to improve my appearance. Jane, I think you'd be better off if you also clean yourself up a bit. But Professor you'd be better off staying scruffy, we don't wanna give the game away, do we?"

"Right, okay then," I replied. I looked towards Max and he was really worried, he wasn't sure the plan would work and who could blame him?

When we were ready Louis, or I should say Louise led the way. The crow didn't recognise him as being male and amazingly he got in with no trouble. After all that moaning and panic, the plan worked like a charm, it was easy...

Whilst Louis was getting ready he mumbled to me about how awful his youth used to be because he had a girl's name. He said that it probably improved him as a mouse, but if he could relive those times again as a normal mouse, he would. I walked in next, closely followed by the shaking Professor. Fortunately the large swirly-eyed crow on the door didn't notice and we entered a new chapter of weirdness...

5. Electro-Thought-Method

Louis led the way through the bizarre entrance and down a twisty tunnel. It had swirly marks on its ceiling and odd wobbly walls that looked like they were made of feathers. He pushed a circular door which distorted like a camera shutter, revealing a large opening inside this funny place

There were no windows at all and the place was lit only by artificial Orange Energy. This came in the form of large flames burning out of two matching pots. These pots were either side of a scruffy looking throne. Two large, pink elephants stood on their hind legs next to these pots and appeared to coax the flames with their trunks. High above us we could see a painting on the ceiling, depicting a hamster whose right paw was reaching out and touching the paw of another hamster. It was all very odd.

Anyway, also close to the painting there was a cage standing on a floating platform. It looked similar to the type of platform that those strange rats had had. It was tricky to make out but it definitely looked like Jim's pecan splint was up there; but where was he? Then, horrible visions entered my brain. I imagined he had he been sacrificed before we had arrived. We all stood there for a few minutes marvelling, in awe of this weird world that we'd found, when suddenly, out of nowhere, we heard a murmur. We looked all around but saw no one.

"I don't like it here," whispered the Professor.

"Nor me," I squeaked.

"Thinking.... I wonder...?" Louis was strolling about talking to himself, when suddenly the murmur turned into an audible sentence...

"Hello, and who might you three be?" a strange voice said. It echoed across the hall in front of us. We looked all around but saw no one.

"Why are you all so dirty? Are you with the other dirty one? Oh wait, you can't be because he's a mouse, or can you?"

"Who's saying that?" Louis screamed in a female voice.

"It's me...." Jim stepped out from behind the throne, he had a large silver ring forced onto his head. He spoke, yet the voice seemed to be from someone or something else. Had he been somehow possessed? That was how it seemed. Suddenly a silver screen appeared from nowhere, and with a puff of smoke a wrinkly, wizened old hamster materialized before us.

Jim's mouth started twitching and then he spoke, "I am speaking through your friend. My name is MacDrid. I came from Scotland many years ago. I can no longer speak without assistance. My voice, my throat, has died in my old hamster body, you see. I have placed this silver ring around your friend's head, it allows me to control his brain. It uses Electro-Thought-Method (ETM). Have you heard of it? Anyway, although your friend is very small, a brain that works is better than a brain that's dead." The wizened MacDrid staggered slightly as he finished speaking.

"Are you okay?" asked Louis, still using his female voice.

"Yes, sort of."

"You can't keep Jim's body. It's a nasty body. Have you heard of the Collective? This hamster I'm with is RedBush," Louis pointed at the disguised Professor, "and he is looking for a church."

"Yes, I know RedBush, but why is he so small? I can tell you why... that is Crimson... and he is a traitor... my son DaVid told me he has the Rodent Key...Where is it, Crimson?"

"Hidden," mumbled the disguised, shaking Professor.

MacDrid waved his hands towards the ceiling and dark shapes began to come to life. A nest of three black round-faces swooped towards us. They landed inches from our feet. They were huge, maybe ten times our size, but they didn't attack. They had the same swirly eyes as the crows and elephants and, now that I came to think of it, as Jim.

"If you look carefully Jane," whispered Louis, "all of these creatures are controlled by that silver ring on their heads. If we can find the device that works it, then they'll be free."

"The creatures may wake and attack us," replied the Professor. Louis sighed. He hadn't thought of that and for once he was without a plan.

"We are meeting the Collective and we need to find their location," stated the Professor.

"They meet often near my church," said MacDrid.

"If you are the king can you tell us the location of this church?" asked the Professor. "If you can we'll give you a reward."

What was happening? Usually it was Louis who bargained or reasoned with our enemies, but now, my friend Max was showing to me, to Louis, and to MacDrid that he too had a presence and an ability to plan.

"And what reward can you possibly give me?" asked MacDrid.

"Dark Energy," the Professor said. "The ability to see and speak without silver discs and a way to bring your real body back to life."

"Strange, you are trying to bargain with me in my home…"

"Do you agree?" asked the Professor. He began to sweat and this caused Crimson's hat to fall from his head. The heat inside the silver cube intensified the more MacDrid used his ETM device and it may have given the hamster a way of attack. But through luck rather than judgement, MacDrid failed to notice.

"I need to discuss the problem with my friends," mumbled Louis. He had joined in the conversation at last. Yet he spoke as a male mouse. Had he forgotten his plan? He'd saved his sweaty friend at his moment of need, or had he?

"Problem? Problem?" giggled MacDrid, "then I have another solution for you my foolish friends. I shall keep all of you as my slaves instead." We turned around and felt the beaks of the round faces at our shoulders. We were taken, one at a time to the cage where Jim's splint was. The Professor slung us his sack of inventions before the round faces led his dirty body over to MacDrid. Then the evil hamster prised the silver ring off Jim's head and placed it over the Professor's. Jim was scooped up, alas unconscious, and dropped into the cage with us. I say dropped, as he literally fell on my body causing slight bruising. I brushed my tubby friend down and smiled, for although he wasn't awake I could feel his heart racing and I knew that he was still alive.

"What are we to do Louise?" I asked.

"Well you can start by calling me Louis. I can't believe I could have been so stupid. It was all a trap, a set up by that crow at the door. Now we've traded the clever Professor, who has still got the magic juice in that locket, for the dim Jim. What a mistake!"

"Well thanks for the insult Louis," groaned Jim. He'd woken and started his first argument for ages. "But don't you see, you need to make mistakes so that you can learn not to do things like that again. Do you remember what the Ssssylfia said?

It said, wipe the smoke from his eyes to discover a wondrous surprise, and do things your way, learn from mistakes and believe in the dreams that you know are not fakes. Don't you see? You're learning to understand the Sacred Scrolls almost to the point that you could write them."

"Yes Jim, maybe you're right."

"So," sighed Jim.

"So we need to escape! But first I need to know how you met MacDrid? Oh, and I noticed that you're no longer hobbling, why, what happened? Does he know a cure?"

"Well it's a long story Louis but here goes…"

"Wait!" I squawked. "Look down there, the Professor's helping that vet hamster with an experiment, what is it?"

"I dunno Jane. We'll find out soon enough no doubt," moaned Jim. He wasn't happy at all that I had butted in on his conversation. "Anyway, as I was saying, this crow… actually, do you see that really big one over there." Jim pointed to an enormous crow perched on the trunk of the left-hand elephant.

"Yeah," we whispered together.

"That crow, it took me inside here to meet MacDrid, who was lying on a bed of strawberries. Anyway, he offered me eternal life if I took part in an experiment. I guess the Professor's a wiser mouse than me. Actually, I wish Crimson Pigs hadn't died then we'd have a joker up our sleeves. It's a shame he's dead, although Max wearing his clothes does look at bit like him, doesn't he?"

"Yes! you've got it. We have to convince Ken that the Professor is the spy Crimson Pigs. If this hamster is discovered liaising with Crimson he'll be ruined. Yes that's it. But wait! How will we get Ken to come here? What kind of lure would make Ken come back to the place where he first started?"

"How about a reunion?" I suggested.

"Yes Jane, that's it. This is gonna be very scary for us, unless we....Yes!"

"Well go on then Louis, spit it out, what?" moaned Jim.

"Well, we only invite Ken to the reunion and not Andrew or the Collective. Yes! I can't believe I didn't think of it sooner."

"But how are you to find him when you don't know where he is?" I asked.

"I'll make MacDrid find him for me. Here, pass me the Professor's sack of inventions, I've got an idea...." Louis' mind was flowing and unlike Crimson Pigs, when he had a plan he tended to share it with us. It is written that when the going gets tough, the tough get going. Well, we were definitely getting tougher by the day. It is also written in the scrolls that to make someone jealous is the best form of attack. If we can make Ken jealous of MacDrid he's sure to explode. His aggression will light up the sky. Yes, Louis had a super plan to lure Ken into his trap. The snag was MacDrid was a lonely old hamster and the only hamster to move to this elephant populated area. Well, he was the only hamster that we ever saw there...

"You see this tablet here Jane, that I've taken from the Professor's sack." He reached across and stuck it right under my nose. "This is it, this is the ONE."

"What, as in the ONE we're looking for?"

"Err, maybe it is, yes. I never really thought of it like that. Yes! Maybe the ONE isn't a rodent like us, maybe, just maybe, it's this tablet!"

"So what's the plan?" asked a confused Jim. The petty squabble that he'd had with Louis had receded into his subconscious, for now anyway. It's funny that, how they had stopped fighting now that everything was deadly serious.

"Right," said Louis, "we have to call MacDrid over. Can you do that for me now please Jim and then just listen and learn."

"Right... err, hello! Hello! MacDrid! Could you possibly pop over and we'll have a chat?"

The wizened old hamster raised his head and looked towards us. He stared straight at Jim and looked stunned. But he did totter over. We watched as he struggled along with a walking stick to a large yellow machine. This mechanical beast was a kind of lifting device. He climbed into its metal mouth. He reached his walking stick towards the control panel and pressed a yellow level on the side of it. Sparks of electricity shimmered around him and this mechanical beast elevated him up into the air. He pressed a yellow button when he was level with Jim and it stopped. Myself and Louis hid behind Jim so MacDrid couldn't see us and Jim asked him some questions.

"What do you want mouse?" asked MacDrid. His lips did not move and the voice echoed from the distant Professor 20 feet beneath us. They both wore discs on their heads and MacDrid's eyes, like the Professor's, were all swirly.

"Err, we've, err..." mumbled Jim. He was stunned by MacDrid's unstable condition. He looked sad, and almost in tears as the wizened hamster continued to ask him questions.

"Well?"

"Can you… no… do you miss the hamsters you came to Kennington with?"

"What, do you mean in the beginning?"

"Yeah," muttered Jim.

"Yes mouse, I do. I haven't seen them for a long time."

"How many hamster prodigies were there?" asked Jim. I believe he was trying to humour him. To lead him into a false sense of security.

"There were four of us. Myself, Ken, Andrew Archdeacon and Two Name. I do miss them. I think of them often."

"Who's Two Name?" asked Louis.

"I can't tell you that can I, then again, maybe I will… what happened was that each one of us went our separate ways. We all wanted different things, you see. I wanted a palace here with these elephants and crows. Ken wanted to start his own colony up in North London and Andrew went a bit odd; he left his tower because he started going crazy. He eventually moved to the end-of-the-tracks. The last I heard of him he had become a chef. Two Name was different. He had twin names because although he was known as Paul to mice he was known as Richard to hamsters. Crossbreeds have this control over others. I wish I was a crossbreed." MacDrid sighed. His head drooped slowly and he staggered.

"Two Name is Paul and Richard?" queried Louis.

"Yes, those with two names are unpredictable you see. Paul Richard turned into a kind of hero for all rodents. I realise now that he had to do what he had to do. He wasn't the kind of creature to listen to other hamsters. You see he was a crossbreed and he defected, he chose to live his life as a mouse. He was the major cause of the break. I remember he went to negotiate a deal with Andrew, but since then I haven't heard anything of him."

"Did he come down from Scotland with you?" Jim asked.

"Yes, well, not directly. Our forefathers have a lot to answer for."

"How many forefathers are there?" asked Jim. I thought this was a stupid question. Surely Jim knew that the forefathers must be four fathers!

"Six," said MacDrid.

"Six?" I yelled, "how can forefathers be six fathers? I don't understand."

"Shhh mouse! You cannot change where you're from but you can change where you're going. Six forefathers! I know because I've met them."

"Where?" asked Jim.

"I'm not telling you mouse! I may be old and frail, but I am not foolish! Us four prodigy hamsters came from different areas but we have all met the Six. I believe the Archdeacon brothers, although they lived in different Scottish towns masterminded operations. Let me tell you about myself. My mother was Spanish and Spain is a warm country. But due to my grape eating fixation I was smuggled out of the country and awoke in the freezing White Lands of Greenock. I was trained at the Morton Rodent Academy. This involved hill walking, racing and scratcher scrapping. Apparently jerboa's like Spain but hamsters prefer the cold, so I went back to my father's roots in Fife."

"I am listening, honest," yawned Jim. He lay on the ground, tummy up and said he was listening with his eyes closed. "Zzzzz... carry on... carry... on..."

"Anyway," said MacDrid, "I believe old hamsters should retire to warmer climes and Two Name suggested London. A built up city like that is much warmer you see. Scotland, although very beautiful with its rolling hills, hides windy storms. It is tricky for a hamster to keep warm and we end up eating all of our stored food. Yes, I have these storage facilities in my cheeks but I have grown old and weary and find hunting for food a chore. I eat most of my food through a straw now, but I miss the warm stories of Spain. A beautiful country I am told, or so my mother said on her death bed. You see, I've never left London since the move from Scotland. I'm a prisoner here now and I shall no doubt die here. I have created this cavern of electrical heat. I like the warmth I have in here. I have my own artificial light in here too. I no longer rely on the White Energy that warms this world. There were of course other hamsters that came down with us from Scotland, but don't get me wrong, we were the captains of our own areas. Oh it brings the memories back to me, but why do you ask me such questions? Do you want to trade something?"

"Not a trade as such, you see we know of Ken. We have seen him. We need to meet with him. We have something he wants," said Louis.

Jim though, had dozed off. He had been listening to start with but he gave the game away when he started to snore. "Zzzzz…Zzzzz,"

"What do you have?" asked MacDrid.

"We have the Rodent Key," gloated Louis.

"The key, you have it? You must give it to me, I need it more."

"Perhaps, but if you send for Ken we can sort this out together, we will never let you have it without Ken. You see we've hidden it." Louis emptied his pockets but as he did so the hazelnut flew out and bounced and rolled towards MacDrid's throne.

"What's that?" asked MacDrid, "Was that the key? I will inspect that shortly…." He turned towards his most loyal crow and said, "Get that funny nut, I must see it."

"Damn," whispered Louis and then yelled towards MacDrid "It's nothing."

MacDrid looked sad. Then, all of sudden he spoke of finding Ken at the church were he hangs out. "I shall send my best crow to bring Ken here. He will bring him by dawn tomorrow, make sure you're awake." And with that MacDrid lowered the lift and went over to inspect the hazelnut.

He stood by his crow and picked it up. He shook it, nothing happened. He licked it, sniffed it and then smiled. We watched as he walked to what looked like an operating table and waved towards the dark round faces. They flew towards him, he whispered something in their pointed ears and they left the silver cube via an emergency hatch way up in the rafters.

"It worked Louis," I whispered. "But what makes you think Ken won't side with this vet?"

"I'm gambling he doesn't." Louis looked more worried than ever. All his hairs were puffed up. It was as though he were trying to look larger than he was. Why was this?

"Why are you puffing yourself out?" I asked.

"Oh I'm just practicing. You see hamsters like a challenge, you know that don't you Jim." Louis flicked Jim's ears and woke our dopey friend up.

"Ow! Oh, what? ….oh yeah, so?"

"So I'm gonna give him one."

A sprightly Jim then said, "Louis! Just because you beat me in a fight when I slept doesn't mean you'll beat the hard hamster Ken, there is no medicine that can treat death you know."

"I'm not gonna fight him with my fluffy paws Jim. It is written that when the belly is full the bones will be at rest."

"So, you're gonna feed him then, is that it?" Jim was sitting by the edge of the cage looking down. He looked sad. He had big bags of flabby flesh under his eyes. It looked as though he hadn't slept properly for a week. He also looked really hungry. Well we all were. What was Louis talking about? How were we gonna feed big Ken when there was no food for ourselves?

"It is also written that wise mice have their mouths in their hearts whilst hamsters have their hearts in their mouths," roared Louis. He had his arms aloft as usual.

"You're getting all philosophical all of a sudden, why? Why can't you tell me how are you're gonna feed him when you can't feed yourself?" complained Jim again.

"I know you're angry. We all are. Look let's get some sleep, tomorrow's going to be a hard day."

That was it, as soon as Louis stopped ranting we all closed our eyes. We were out like lights, before the count started…

6. Secret Transformation

The definition of the count being MacDrid's early morning chanting.... "One, two, three, go!..........Yes! One, two, three, go!.......Got it again! Ha! Ha!"

The chatter below us became louder and louder. I woke up first, then Louis. I guess it was a kind of fitness exercise for the mind of MacDrid. He was inside the Professor with his words of confusion. The lame body of the real vet was slumped on the throne struggling to eat some grapes. It looked as though his real body was too weak to pull the grapes from the stalks. It was a sad sight, especially at five in the morning.

"What we've gotta do is this, oh hang on, Jane, wake Jim up will you please."

"Sure," I replied. I put my left paw over his mouth before I tickled him, this saved him from squealing and sending a siren of alert over towards MacDrid. Jim wriggled a bit and opened his eyes, but they were stuck together. He said that as he was so tired sleepy-eye-syndrome had taken over, so although he seemed awake he couldn't see.

"Right Jim, I've dipped into the Professor's sack and this tablet is for your use. You have to stay up here alone while myself and Jane try to free the Professor. We're gonna try and get the silver disc off his head when Ken and the wizened vet are fighting. But it will be tight for a time so watch yourself. Oh yeah, don't use the tablet until you're absolutely ready, okay."

"What tablet, I can't see, I'm too tired."

"Look!..." squeaked Louis as he slapped Jim across the face and then frantically licked him.

"Mmmmm...mmm," mumbled Jim. Louis had covered his mouth to stop him from squeaking and all I could hear was murmured sighs.

"Gotcha!" squeaked Louis and he climbed on top of his dopey friend. "This tablet will change into two Max-Puppets. One will look like me and the other like Jane. You'll have to climb up and control them both by the strings above them. Don't do it too badly and only do it if the vet wants to talk with me."

"That's the weirdest plan yet Louis," I squeaked.

"Madness," complained Jim, who was now awake and fiddling with his whiskers. Louis then stuffed Max-Cotton-Wool balls into Jim's mouth, but he spat them out. "Urrr! What are you doing?"

"Put them back; that the cotton wool in your mouth will disguise your voice," grinned Louis as he winked at me.

"You do have odd plans I'll give you that," I whispered.

"We won't be too long I hope, and Jim, we're counting on you okay."

Louis opened the sack again and pulled out another tablet, he licked it and it changed into a Max-Rope. I watched as he tied it to the edge of the cage and swung the other end to a post.

Louis went first and I followed him down. It made a change for me not to be the look out and to be on a mission. I was crawling along behind Louis but he wasn't happy with my attitude. I felt like I had been promoted but I knew that in his eyes my help may only hinder his plan, sadness.

THIS PUPPET IDEA IS HARDER THAN IT LOOKS

"Jane, shhhhh! We have to scamper quietly." We sneaked along. Louis told me to leave a five foot gap between us. He'd run a bit, give me the all clear, then I'd join him. We did this all the way across the floor. We must have run past at least five chairs and two tables. Then in the corner of the room we could see the athletic body of our friend moving about. We watched as Max, still wearing the silver disc, placed the hazelnut into a metal container. Max then switched a big machine on and a roar came from it. He then attached two long grabbers.

"What are those?" I whispered to Louis.

"I'm not sure."

Max then attached a coiled wire and dripped tiny drops of magical juice from the locket onto the hazelnut. He walked towards a socket switch and turned it on. A sweeping bolt of blue electricity glistened along the coiled wire and reacted with the hazelnut, but nothing happened.

Then we saw the wizened MacDrid walk to the table, but he seemed unhappy. Max took the hazelnut out of the metal container and handed it back to MacDrid. The hamster sniffed it again, sighed, struggled back to his throne and fell asleep.

"What's going on?" I asked Louis.

"Shhh! I don't know... actually Jane I've got a new plan. We'll have to get into a position to tease the vet hamsters' wizened body.... look over there!" He pointed towards the left-hand elephant and it too was asleep. It's head was flat on the floor and yet it's body was still sitting upright.

"Okay, now what,"

"Shhh! If we run up the trunk and onto its right tusk we'll be level with MacDrid's face. Come on, let's go, there's no time to lose..." I followed Louis on his mad scampering mission.

I remember looking back and seeing Jim waving at me in the distance and he looked so small; I guess it was because he was so far away. Then suddenly everything went black and I found myself in a slimy tunnel. I stopped running and became scared. Louis wasn't with me, so where was he? Had he deserted me? And then, weirdly, I couldn't smell him. I turned around and saw a light at the end of the tunnel. I forced my way along the hairy corridor treading over sticky rocks and feeling my way along nasty crusty walls until I reached the light source. Then the strangest think happened: as I came out of the tunnel I noticed Louis with his paws on his hips. It seemed he was tapping his left foot on the ground and shaking his head. Also his facial characteristics had changed, just like MacDrid said they would. What was wrong with him?

You RAN INSIDE ITS NOSE, YUK!

"Come on Jane, a little bit further. Here, give me your left paw." I reached out towards him and touched his fingers. They seemed moist. As he pulled me out I panicked. I realised that I had accidently run up the inside nostril of this enormous elephant's nose.

"Urrr! It's horrible in there."

"Jane, please spare me the details."

I again followed Louis. This time I was concentrating. It is written that it's better to keep your mouth and dreams shut and your eyes open.

We made it to the tusk quite easily and although Louis said it was a slippery surface and tricky to climb I was okay. Why? Because my feet were sticky from that nostril and I had excellent grip.

"I think we should hide in this ear and wait for the dawn to break," suggested Louis.

"The dawn?" I asked. I was confused by Louis' use of words.

"Yes! We must wait until the sun rises properly. Now as it's only five in the morning it doesn't really count. When the sun comes up, the morning will be ready and waiting and then Ken should arrive."

"It's gonna be a hard day today isn't it?"

"Yes Jane. In our history in this new world we can see that today, actually, this morning, will be the big one for us!"

"Is this big one similar to the *ONE* we seek?"

"I dunno. We'll just have to wait and see...."

There was still no sign of Ken being early so we waited. As myself and Louis tucked ourselves down deep into the ear we both knew our destiny was waiting for us out there, somewhere..

I was awake and sitting with Louis in the ear of one of MacDrid's elephants. I had already run up the trunk into its sticky tunnel and now I waited with Louis for the arrival of the nasty cousin of MacDrid- the horrid Ken Archdeacon.

MacDrid had said his cousin would arrive at dawn. It was strange sitting in that ear and waiting. For although we were in MacDrid's secret world we had no natural light inside, only his artificial Orange Energy light.

"I have a question Louis, as something is confusing me. How do we know when dawn is if we have no way of seeing dawn inside this silver chamber?" But Louis ignored me, sadness. It wasn't that he was being selfish, it was because most of my previous questions had easy answers but this one made him think.

"Good question, let me see… I remember, I remember, the prison where I was born, the little wheel that caught the sun, that came peeping in at dawn," he chanted. He was whispering of course, he didn't want to wake the elephants or we'd have been an irritation and maybe been crushed to death. Louis continued with his odd speech and I just listened still squashed under his body. "I remember, I remember, when I first glimpsed your smile, in the forest late at night when moths and flies came to life and fluttered around a while."

"What?" I asked.

"I was just reminiscing, thinking about when I first met you Jane. It seems so long ago."

"Yes, and so much has happened. Eon, who I have known all my life has flown from the nest. The Professor believes his long lost stepbrother Paul is a pecan, but now it seems he might be a crossbreed with two names instead. Jim's been with us from the start, yet he's always been so distant in his convictions. I believe he's too selfish. It scares me Louis. We've done many things and yet I still feel I don't know enough."

"Calm down," whispered Louis, "maybe a simple, logical solution is staring us in the face and we just can't see it."

"Sorry Louis, changing the subject, earlier you spoke of moths, those fat flying creatures, didn't you. I never did like moths really. They always home in on the lights don't they, yet you never see them in the day. Where do they go?"

"That's it Jane! Yes! If we can simulate light MacDrid will be under our control. His crows understand when the real dawn outside is here but he relies on them to tell him. If we can convince these crows we'll be in control." Louis began to glow again. The possibility of a solution was apparent. But how was he gonna change the way of the world? Inside this large silver cube there were no windows. I often wondered how MacDrid knew about dawn if he'd not been out for ages.

"How will he know when it's dawn?" I asked.

"The crows inform him somehow. I think he goes by the reflections in their eyes. If they show signs of light it must be light outside." Louis pointed towards a cluster of nests. "Look up there Jane! That's the home of the crows. If we can somehow light them, they'll glow like a sun, like a dawn sun."

Louis was concentrating hard and unlike Crimson he'd explained the plan rather than risk our lives without a just cause or explanation.

I started to daydream about Crimson again because he did tell me things, but it was as if he didn't want Louis to know them. Crimson told me once that the night sky was a cluster of tiny stars but that in reality they weren't as tiny as he had once thought. It was their distance from us that made them small rather than their actual size. He said all stars are like our Sun, that glowing energy that warms our world, but life was created by Dark Energy. He said all the stars have there own planets just like ours, yet some are tiny and some are huge. He said the standard shape of a planet is round and it can be made of different elements. Elements are nothing like elephants and can be different gases or rock formations or types. He confused me a lot and now he's gone. He was the cleverest rodent that I'd ever met but his lack of teamwork eventually killed him. Louis was right, he was a fool.

"If White Energy is daytime, is Dark Energy night time?" I asked. I was confused by this world and by how we were alive, capable of thought, yet plants and concrete rivers were not.

"I cannot confirm your theory although it does seem to me to be a good theory," sighed Louis. He was always like that with me, although his theory was worse than mine. He suggested that the Dark Energy manipulates the Sun to rise in the morning and set in the evening.

"Our Sun commands our Moon Jane, when we are outside again I will show you this round blob that only comes out of hiding when our Sun is sleeping."

He assumes this Sun supervises our Moon and this in turn controls our seas and oceans using gravity and forces connected to our world. He said the Sun and its position in the sky controls the climates, the temperatures and that this fantastic star was one of millions in the sky. I remember once he pointed to them and suggested that as there were so many stars there must be other worlds out there similar to our own. His knowledge was different to Crimson's but at least he shared his theories and, unlike Crimson, he was still alive.

The Ssssylfia; the manifestation, or ghost, or smoke as Jim calls it, must be connected to Dark Energy. It is a substance that cannot be seen yet is all around. Yet, with the Ssssylfia we do see an image, so maybe it is just a pointer in the right direction rather than the answer.

"I was thinking Louis, maybe this Dark Energy controls our emotions and instincts. To be able to think and search and imagine stuff aren't things that are visible yet we still have them. Or maybe danger is Dark Energy as without it we would surely be non existent and never want to progress and evolve."

"Interesting when you think about stuff isn't it. You could think about a whole world of different things such as why unpredictables wear clothes, or why we were born as mice, why trees are green, why rivers are blue and why hamsters control London or even what creature is inside that hazelnut? The list of questions is endless." Louis looked towards me and smiled. I think I'd finally matured in his eyes. I was becoming the kind of mouse that he wanted me to be.

We both clambered down in front of the sleeping MacDrid so that we had a good view of the nests. Louis started rummaging around in his invention sack again. I say 'his' because he still believed it must originally have been Crimson's, not the Professor's. Actually, a striking thought had just dawned on me (a different kind of dawn). The inventions are… I'll ask Louis I think, that's what I'll do. "Louis! Louis! Don't most of the inventions that you get out of the sack have the Professor's name on?"

He looked down onto the tablets and there, engraved across each one, was 'MAX'. "Err, yes! Yes, they must be his then." He looked sad again. He always looked sad when he'd been proved wrong.

My thoughts had overcome my fears. I always knew it wasn't right for him to keep on calling the Professor a liar and a thief. I guess Louis owes him an apology now. I also guess he won't tell him unless he can save him. I just hope he gives more than 100% if that's possible.

I was becoming agitated, after my praise for Louis' communication skills he wasn't telling me this plan! "What do you want to do? What are you looking for? Don't be like Crimson and not say... what's the plan?"

"Jane please be patient. I've found a suitable tablet I think." He licked it and it changed into a Max-Bow and Arrow. He pulled out another tablet and licked that as well. This one turned into a match.

"What are they for?"

"Shhhh! Come over here Jane." I walked towards him. "Hold this arrow," he said passing me the match at the same time. He then tied one of the tissue pieces that we had used during our escape from that prison in Clapham all that time ago, onto the end of the arrow.

"I don't understand," I mumbled.

"Right, now strike the match on the ground and light the end of the arrow with the tissue."

The match flared into life.

WHOOSH! It went, and I lit the tissue, he then took aim. He pulled the elastic section of the bow and fired towards the nests...

It worked. He struck first go. He was a mouse so full of surprises.

"Come on Jane, this way.." He led us back into the ear of the elephant and we waited. It was sticky inside that ear but not as bad as its trunk. We sat, our heads peeping out, and watched as bits of nest and then wooden beams thundered loose and started falling to the ground all around us.

The noise and the heat awoke the largest crow I'd ever seen. It flew high above the smouldering nests and opened the hatch.

"Look Louis! It's still dark outside."

"Yes, but..." he pointed to a giant raven as it flew through the hatch and towards MacDrid, "that beast has a message tied to its leg. But where was Ken?"

The raven also had swirly eyes and I watched with my heart in my mouth as Louis sneaked along and gently untied the message and placed it in his pocket. Then a terrible fight occurred between the crow and the raven.

Then wooden beams from the rafters crackled as they burned and charred pieces fell to the ground. The fight ended and the raven flew off leaving the crow half-dead on the ground. Louis sneaked over to MacDrid, but the hamster lay motionless. He nudged him but MacDrid just toppled off his throne into a heap. What had happened? Was he really dead? Louis pointed to large beams from the rafters lying next to MacDrid's body. It looked as though, while we were watching the fighting, MacDrid had met his death. We then started to hear a murmuring sound coming from the other elephant. It had a familiar voice and was in distress.

"Help me! I'm getting squashed!" said the voice.

"Who said that?" asked Louis.

"I dunno," I replied and pointed to the grey beast, "it came from that elephant, I think."

We rushed to the back of the beast and we could just about see the Professor's head sticking out, but his body was crushed underneath. He'd managed somehow to save the locket. It was a bizarre sight. It was the first time I'd ever seen an elephant in such an unusual position.

"What can we do Louis? He's gonna die if we don't rescue him?" I screamed. Then out of the corner of my eye I noticed

Jim. He appeared to be shouting at us, but because of the hassles we faced we ignored his cries...

"Hey!" screamed Jim again. We still didn't respond. Louis had a look on his face that told you what he was thinking. I guess he thought Jim would ask a silly question, or do a stupid trick. "Hey! I can help! Hey!" Still Louis ignored him, but his persuasive chatter finally cracked my hardened shell.

"Hey! Jane! Toss me the sack, quickly!"

"Okay..." I squeaked. I did what Jim wanted, I ran towards him and threw it up and then scurried back to help the Professor.

Louis was annoyed that I had taken the sack away from him whilst he was attempting to save our crushed friend. I looked up, and high in the distance I noticed Jim poking around in the sack, he was looking for something.

"I've got it!" Jim shrieked. He produced a Max-Spider and threw it towards the elephants. They both jumped to their feet and knocked the metal container holding the hazelnut. It rolled out, looked up and shot across the floor; it then ran off down a mouse hole. I couldn't believe what I had seen.

"Did you see that?" I said to Louis.

"What?" he snarled.

"That hazelnut, I think it's alive."

"Don't be silly? We need to get out of here." He grabbed the worn out looking Professor. "Head for that mouse hole... come on... quickly... do you want me to do everything?"

High above us the nests were burning more than ever and pieces of smouldering wood began to fall all around us. Louis was right we had to get out. Jim climbed down the Max-Rope that we'd left there and followed us down the disused mouse hole. Inside there was a warm breeze blowing. Then I saw Jim grab something.

"What's this?" he mumbled to himself.

We scurried along, panicking. As we reached the end of the twisty tunnel we emerged onto a new higher level, this one was called Elephant's Castle. We of course knew why.

"So now what Louis?" asked a filthy Jim.

"Now we go to see Ken at his church."

And that was that. MacDrid had died, his silver cube castle had burnt to a crisp because of us and Jim had found something but wouldn't say what.

Our mission continued. We now had to meet with the evil hamster Ken Archdeacon who had failed to turn up to meet his cousin. We had set up this meeting because we didn't know where his church was; we still don't. I wonder why he didn't come?

Can you trust Living Dust...?

1. Hamster Code

Dark Energy holds many answers and many possible explanations. I believe the Rodent Key is not an explanation, it merely opened the faith safe containing the Dark Matter. But DM is a substance that can be seen whereas Dark Energy, as the Ssssylfia has told us, cannot be seen. It is possible though that the key may open other doors for us, doors we have not yet discovered...

I really feel that if we give the Rodent Key to Ken we will be sacrificing our future. We've tried to find Max's stepbrother Paul who the Professor believes has been transformed into a pecan by Andrew Archdeacon, using the DM tablets. But now we have discovered from a ranting, sad MacDrid that Paul is known as Two Name and is a crossbreed, being half-hamster and half-mouse! We had, up to that moment, believed Paul was a mouse; but in reality it now appeared that he was a spy, working for our enemies and was actually named Richard. But more amazingly, Richard is allegedly 2nd in line to the throne of Jerboa. So this poses a new question. Why are Paul Richard and our leader Louis both in line to a throne of a jerboa? If either of them were jerboas I would understand it. But as they are not, maybe we need to trace the six Scottish forefathers to understand this riddle. But we had so many things to do and so little time. It just makes the Dark Energy search appear less important. I don't understand what's happening anymore. Everything is becoming too complex. Everything is making my mind seize up. I can't continue like this. I am confused as to our purpose and think that we need to at least speak to the camouflaged rats properly to fully understand what the point of our existence is…

"Let's go and find Ken," said Louis.

"But we don't know where he is do we?" Jim replied. He sulked on the floor next to the Professor. They looked dreadful. The Professor's rear legs were really badly bruised and Jim's morale was very low. I didn't have the heart to tell him what his whiskers looked like!

"I do, well sort of," answered Louis. We all stood shivering as he dipped his hand into his pocket and pulled out the note that he had taken from that raven's leg at MacDrid's castle. "Look I'll read it out… oh no… it's written in Hamster code."

"What a mess! So what do you make of it? That's a sign of a rushing hamster if you ask me," sighed the Professor. "The only way I can translate that message is using an invention; now where's my sack?" And then he saw it, squashed deep into Louis' furry pocket. He ran towards him and snatched it back.

"Swine," muttered Louis, but we all knew that he was the swine not the Professor. "All Max will do is translate the code, I don't see what all the fuss is about. I've had that sack a long time... but... well... oh it doesn't matter."

"All Louis! All! That's a tricky job that is," moaned Jim. He was speaking while at the same time fiddling with his whiskers. It looked like he was picking the dirt from their roots.

The Professor stood in front of us and selected a suitable tablet and began mumbling to himself as he sifted through them. "These tablets are getting quite low, I have to use this MIN one instead, damn." But Louis was hassling him while he was trying to imagine his Max-Translator, and this upset his rhythm. "Stop getting in the way Louis, oh no... the tablet has changed into a device but it doesn't look right. "

"What's the problem?" I asked.

"There are certain symbols that don't translate at all. And others that don't make sense. I don't understand?"

"Well I do," moaned Jim. "You said yourself that hamsters can't spell so Hamster code won't be any better will it. Just try to get the gist of what it says."

"Okay," replied the Professor. "Yes well, it sort of says something about a cross. As a hunch I think we need to go to the town called King's X. Look at that unpredictable map on the wall, can you see if a King's X is on there."

"Yeah there is one," grinned Jim, "maybe you're right. Look, there's a mechanical beast, let's jump on."

Jim led the way for a change. We all followed. Jim liked being in control. Maybe he was destined for greater things. The beast stopped in Kennington. It seemed to be going the wrong way but before we could jump off it started moving again.

"You've led us the wrong way Jim, you fool!" cursed the Professor.

"Well I didn't know did I? I'm not a compass. I don't know which way is right, it's...it's...just...oh nothing." He started to sulk by the bumper on his own. For about two minutes he had been happy, but mistakes are there to be made in the land of confusion. The beast pulled into the next higher level and this time we were ready to jump off as Louis took over command and led the way.

"Come on all of you!" shouted Louis but his yelling attracted the attention of an ear-ringed unpredictable. We all ran under one of the chocolate machines in an attempt to hide. Alas the unpredictable crouched down in front of us and tried to grab us. He thrust his hand and arm deep underneath. His fingers reached to within millimetres of my fluffy brow. He had a strange kind of mechanism attached to his wrist which the Professor said was similar to his Max-Clock.

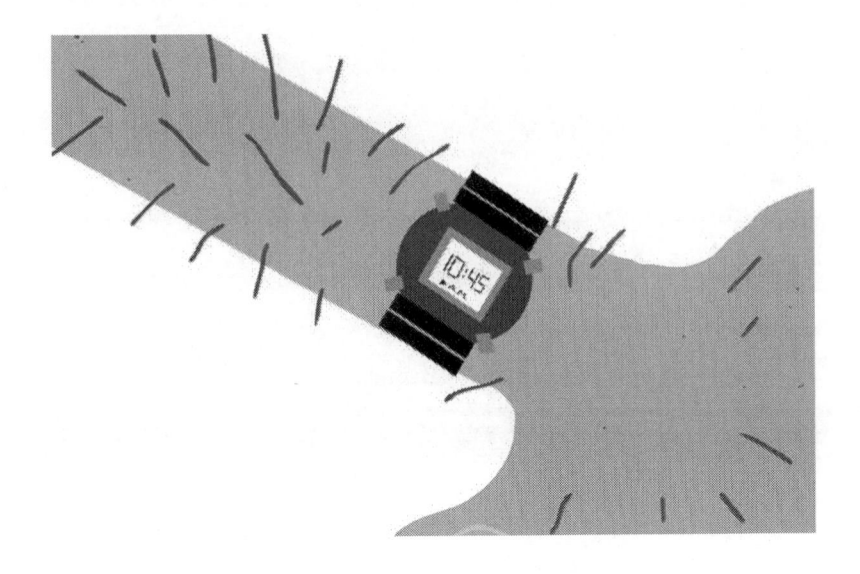

"The unpredictables call these things watches. But this one is bizarre. It's a digital type made of Lithium crystals," whispered the Professor.

The time read 10:45 and the watch had a little indicator on it that pointed to the letters: a.m. "What do those letters mean Louis?" I asked.

"I dunno."

"I do," said the Professor, "a.m. means ante meridiem. A.M. or ante meridiem means morning time, as in before noon. It comes from an ancient unpredictable language called Latin. You see those other letters there: p.m.- they mean the opposite, as in post meridiem, that's after noon. If we need to see Ken at this King's X place by 12pm we've got just over one hour to get there!"

Suddenly the bright lights of the mechanical beast lit us up and the unpredictable could see us, but instead of grabbing us he scurried off and climbed on board. Luckily we were safe as he'd given up and gone.

"Wow that was close. Max, I didn't know you were that clever, I'm impressed," said Jim, eagerly, "but what unusual gift should we bring on MacDrid's behalf, I mean his cousin will expect something won't he?"

"Stop babbling… look, over there…" screamed Louis. He pointed to the mechanical beast as it disappeared down another tunnel and we watched as the Ssssylfia emerged from the blackness once more.

> Look all around see what's able
> Try to understand my fable
> Watch my mist drift over ground
> Watch it hover, see what you've found
> Is it luck that you'll get it right?
> Or is the simple answer clear
> Will you understand your fear?

"What is that Ssssylfia on about?" asked Jim. He slumped on the ground and then, as usual started moaning, "I will never understand this smoke! It talks more rubbish than you Louis!"

We all just looked at each other. Then we watched the Ssssylfia almost shrug its shoulders (if it had shoulders) in disbelief as it drifted across the higher level in front of us before disappearing again back into the blackness...

2. The Morning of the Roundish Table

"We need to read into its wisdom," answered Louis. "Ssssylfia speaks for longer each time. It's trying desperately to help us. Luck must be on our side."

"Well we'll need it won't we because we haven't got much else!" moaned Jim.

"Shhh! It speaks of luck, of simple things. The answer must be here at this higher level. Look at the title of it, its name, it says: OVAL."

"Do you really think that's relevant?" quizzed Jim.

"Yes I do. Look, in the Ssssylfia's first line it instructed us to look all around. Don't you see, 'OVAL', 'AROUND', is there a connection with this place? There must be!" Louis was focusing hard on the words. The rest of us couldn't really understand the logic behind the Ssssylfia riddles. To us they seemed silly.

"I don't get it at all," moaned Jim.

"Look! The Ssssylfia spoke of itself drifting over the ground, then it asked us what we'd found. Now we haven't found anything yet but… oh… look over there!" Louis pointed to an unpredictable carrying a round parcel. As another mechanical beast arrived the unpredictable entered it and accidently left his object behind. Was this fate? Is this what the

Ssssylfia predicted would happen? We all scampered over to get a closer look.

"It's round alright but enormous," squeaked Jim.

"It's not round, it's kind of oval," grumped the Professor.

"Yes, well, roundish isn't it. I think we should carry this to King's X," replied Louis. He had a strength in his face, his eyes. He could have crushed us with a single stare. When I say us, I'm not counting Jim of course.

"Look at the size of it, you must be out of your tiny mind. The weight of that will crush us for sure. You've lost it, that's what you've done. Louis, you've gone mad. It must be this place, the warmth in the air, the breath of the unpredictables, it's all confused your ideas. Think before you speak. Is it not written that we are born crying, live complaining and die disappointed. Your ideas aren't real Louis, your foolish ideas will be the end of us all." Jim collapsed into a ball on the ground. Tears poured from his fluffy face. A large pool gathered around our feet. The Professor tried to comfort him but to no avail.

"Jim! Hey Jim! It is also written that a mouses' wit is in his paws. Watch..." Louis scampered over to the large roundish object. He flicked it with his tail and it crashed to the ground.

THUD!

"What are you doing? What did you do that for?" asked the Professor.

"Watch." Louis grabbed the Professor's sack of inventions and pulled out a tablet. We watched as he licked it twice in quick succession.

"You don't wanna do that you know, if you lick it twice you'll get a double invention," explained the Professor.

"Exactly..."

We all stood a good ten feet away from Louis as he place the tablet next to the edge of the roundish thing. Suddenly the tablet changed into a pair of Max-Roller-Skates. Louis ran towards the chocolate machine and stuck his right paw up the coin rejection compartment. He was making some odd noises. He said, "Got...it...yes...yeah.. got...." after a bit of wriggling his left paw popped out with a lump of gum. It was quite a large lump.

"I saw that ear-ringed unpredictable pop it in there earlier, you know, the ONE that tried to grab us, the ONE that wore that odd wrist thing," said Jim.

"So what do you need that for?" I asked.

"Patience Jane, watch..." He pulled the still soggy gum into two pieces. He then placed one blob on each Max-Roller-Skate.

"Professor! Come over here."

The Professor wandered over, "What?"

"All you've gotta do is keep it balanced," said Louis.

Myself and Jim watched as they hoisted the edge of the object onto the Max-Roller-Skates. One skate at each end.

Then Louis pulled out another tablet. He licked it and it turned into a Max-Jack. It was a device used by unpredictables that to lift their mechanical machines so that they could change the tyres. Louis placed it under the roundish object. He then started pumping on the handle. Basically he was raising the object up. It was the Professor's job to keep it balanced. Eventually they got it totally upright and slid it onto the Max-Roller-Skates, the gum acted as a glue to help hold it in position. Louis went to the front and pulled the Max-Roller-Skate gently and it rolled along.

"That was quite impressive, but pray tell me how will you get it onto the mechanical beast?" Jim was amused by Louis' skills but questioned his capabilities.

"Watch and learn..." When the beast arrived he pulled out a Max-Rope from his pocket. He swung it in the air like a lasso, then let go of the spinning end and it hooked onto the bumper. It was a perfect cowboy's trick.

"Shot, Louis," I screamed.

It was amazing how Louis had again pulled off another trick from his secret skills collection. How could such a young mouse be so talented? He wasn't that much older than me and yet he knew so much more. Is that what happens when you don't listen to what's going on all the time? Why are some mice, who have lived a similar kind of lifestyle to me, more wise to what's going on? This sort of situation annoys me. If only I'd paid attention all those months ago; still Louis is at least on our side so I guess it could be worse.

WHY IS MAX STILL WEARING CRIMSON'S CLOTHES?

NO IDEA!

"Come on everyone!" Louis screamed as he led the way with an air of authority in his teasing chants. "There's only a matter of minutes before we meet Ken. Chop! Chop!"

"All right, all right we're coming, there's no need to shout," Jim snapped. He clambered on last, but because of the roundish object there wasn't very much space for him. He squashed himself into the tiny gap between the back of the beast and the object. "Ow! Argh! Agony!"

"Stop complaining will you please!"

"Look Louis I don't understand why we're bringing this thing all right, come on tell me? Why on earth do we really need to bring something this big?" whinged Jim. I couldn't see his face as he was jammed in the gap with his head pointing inwards.

"Shhh! Jim! Shhh! It is written that beauty is in the eye of the beholder. I think this means that if we give a gift to Ken saying that it's from MacDrid he'll be pleasantly surprised. It is also written that surprise opens the doors to new wonders. If we please Ken he may surprise us back."

"What, like really bringing Richard along?"

"Yes Jim, like that, if it is Richard."

We rushed along past the higher levels. I watched as we passed Elephant Castle, Borough, London Bridge, Monument, Bank, Mor's Gate and the next one we reached was called Old Street.

"Why's this one old because it doesn't look wrinkly?" I asked Louis.

"Because it's been here the longest."

We all watched as the beast came to a stop in London's oldest station. It was a bit of a shock looking at it, as it seemed so clean.

"Look at that unpredictable!" shouted the Professor.

"I can't..." mumbled Jim, "I can't.. get.. my.. head.. round.. that way...". I watched as he pushed and shoved his tubby face in the direction of the higher level, unfortunately though, one of his whiskers got caught on the sticky tape holding the object's wrapping on. "Ow! Oooh! Ow! It's hurting me!"

"Let me try to help," I squeaked as I balanced my tiny frame along the edge of the bumper, I had an area of about one centimetre to walk on.

"Wait! I'm nearer Jane," suggested the Professor. I watched as he dipped his paw into his sack of inventions and pulled out an oblong tablet. We watched as he licked it and it changed into a pair of Max-Choppers. With the care and attention of a surgeon he positioned them near Jim's face. "Jim! Hey Jim! Push the edge over the whisker that's trapped."

"I'm not letting you cut my whisker. I've had that one all my life, I can't let it happen."

We watched as a tear rolled down his face, it reached the said whisker and trickled along it before dripping into the blackness below. I guess it was Jim's way of saying goodbye my friend, it was always fun when you were around.

"Let him do the deed Jim you can always grow another," giggled Louis.

"Louis you swine! That's your answer to everything isn't it. You think that when a loved one is gone it doesn't matter because you've got others, but it does matter see. I hate losing part of me for no reason. Is it not written that whiskers are the backbone of all rodent happiness."

"No it isn't," answered Louis.

"Well maybe it should be! Oh go on then Professor, ruin my life, Louis has been doing it at every opportunity he can get anyway."

"I hope you don't want me to attempt to squeeze into tight places anymore; without my whiskers I won't be able to judge anything." We watched as Jim lined the Max-Choppers up with his prize whisker.

SNIP!

Jim's face fell. He was free but dejected. He stared over towards an unpredictable on the higher level that the Professor had pointed to. We looked towards Jim and then the unpredictable and they looked quite similar in a way. Jim was holding his face, he had tears and anger was written right across it. Whilst the unpredictable rubbed his left hand over his cheeks and appeared to have a slight whisker growth starting. This unpredictable was not on his own, he was with a young abusive female; ear-ringed of course. She looked like she was giving him a hard time. She complained about his whiskers and yet he just stared at her, tears forming in his is eyes. He tried to rub them away but the more he rubbed the more new ones appeared.

"This is a sad higher level isn't it Louis?" I muttered.

"Yes Jane, it is."

"Do you know why?"

"I believe it's the cross over point. You see, although I don't understand the unpredictable way of life, certain areas of this city create different characters. Look... you see that unpredictable there...." he pointed to a really well dressed female of the species. "You see how clean and smart she is, that's critical. Notice she too has earrings but a different type to the ones we're used to seeing. I believe she comes from an area of London where the people are what is known as *'Wealthy'*. You see, there are four sections of London with seven personality areas. This place we've been brought up in is a whole world to us. The condition of these areas is reflected in the unpredictable characters it produces. You see these unpredictables are not all bad. Some of them, the older ones, are really wise. It is written that wisdom sometimes walks in powerful shoes. I take this to mean you can tell an unpredictable's character as much by their shoes as their ear decorations. Anyway, I think the four areas of London are called: North, South, East and West. Now each one of these areas contains unpredictables that fall into seven personality types. Each personality is difficult to establish unless we understand their minds. These seven are: Wealth, Fun, Happiness, Sadness, Bitterness, Anger and Greed. How many more unpredictables are nasty rather than nice?"

"Lots," I mumbled. Alas I was becoming bored and Louis had started one of his babbling trips again; still at least he was happy.

"Correct. So this, I believe, is a significant step towards their origins. Notice how the male unpredictable over there suffers from sadness, yet his so-called friend portrays signs of anger. It is these fundamental mistakes that unpredictables make that will be their downfall. I don't understand why only bad, negative things are highlighted by these bizarre creatures. I thinks it's because they're screwed up inside; I know it sounds sad but it's true. It is written that two wrongs don't make a right. You see Jane, the Sacred Scrolls tell the truth whatever the species. I wonder what that Jerbil MacTaggart rodent was really like?"

"Have you finished babbling, because we're here," snarled Jim. We looked up and saw that we'd reached King's X. Louis led the way as usual and we jumped off.

"Hey Jim! Here's the Rodent Key, you'll have to carry it as myself and the Professor are struggling with this roundish object." Louis threw it towards Jim but he wasn't really paying much attention. "Oi!... Jim!... Catch!"

"What? Ow!" The key struck Jim in the face and disappeared down a hole near the tracks.

"Why you!" Myself and the Professor watched as Louis chased Jim around the higher level before heading back to where the key went.

"Well, it wasn't my fault Louis," moaned Jim.

"It never is, is it!"

"So now what?" we all said together.

We all sat at the edge of the higher level staring into the blackness below. There was an unpredictable sign on the ground which read: *MIND THE GAP* I guess we didn't...

3. The Grubby Sewers

Suddenly we saw a flicker, something fluffy and fluttering, near the mislaid key. The Professor pulled out a Max-Torch from his sack and then another invention, this one being a Max-Fishing-Rod. He tied the Max-Torch to the hook at the end and wound towards the hole. It must have been a bizarre sight to the unpredictables that were waiting for the mechanical beast to arrive.

As the Professor lowered the Max-Torch down the hole the darkness was illuminated and we saw that the flicker of fluff appeared to be a moth.

"Why's there a moth down there Louis?" asked Jim.

"I believe it's an underground city."

"What? Another one? Or is this where the rats live? After all, this is in the hamster town of King's X and they like to play dangerous games here, don't they. Maybe this is where the sewer rats live and fight," suggested the Professor.

"Look at the edges of the hole. There appear to be scuff marks, but not ordinary ones: it looks like... no it can't be... but it is... the marks are cross-shaped. Maybe down there is the true King's X," suggested Louis.

"What on earth is going on?" questioned Jim. He sat on his own by the hole, but not too close, as he was worried that falling down holes seemed to be common practice for mice of his tender years.

"I think the moth is not a moth," said Louis.

"What do you mean?" asked Jim.

"I mean, I believe it's a sign. A sign left for us by the Ssssylfia. Don't you see, a moth lives by light, but I believe that this moth is the light."

"What?" asked Jim.

"It's a symbol of light."

"Look Louis, how can it be light? I'm going down to investigate." And with that Jim grabbed the Max-Torch, jumped into the hole and chased after the moth.

"Come back you fool!" shouted Louis. He turned towards us and said, "is there anybody else who needs to die before they see the truth?"

"Die?" asked myself and the Professor simultaneously.

"Yes die. You see, the light is a glimmer of hope and unless Jim catches that light he's a goner."

"Why?" we asked.

"Because... are you both blind? The Rodent Key has fallen into an unpredictable hole, this hole is occupied by the hope-moth, don't you see? The Rodent Key opened the faith safe, correct?"

"So?" I asked. Louis had started babbling again and in a Crimson-like way he wasn't telling us everything he was thinking.

"What do you mean, 'SO?'"

"What? We don't understand," said the Professor.

"Well... actually, is it not written in the Sacred Scrolls of Jerboa that there are three blind mice! Maybe you two and Jim are those three. Yes! Yes! That would answer many a question about your lack of knowledge."

The Professor turned to me and shrugged his shoulders and then made madness gestures towards Louis, saying, "Jane, maybe Jim's right you know, maybe Louis is mad. Come on let's follow Jim, maybe he is the one doing the right thing."

I watched as Max jumped down the hole too, but as he was gripping my left paw he took me down with him. I remember looking upwards as we headed downwards and I saw Louis' tear-streaked face, it was awful.

"Come back you fools!" Louis was shouting and waving his arms at us, and I had to agree that the Professor was right, he did look mad. "Come back will you! We need to take the round object to Ken! I'll never be able to manage on my own."

"Sorry!" we shouted up to him, as we disappeared into the blackness. The Professor then led me in the direction of the flickering light, the light of hope I guess Louis would call it. We seemed to walk for miles in those sewers, deeper and deeper towards the centre of the earth. There was a nasty pooey smell and a gentle river of stinky water flowing through that murky, unknown, underground world.

4. Howard's Circus Emporium

The Professor then pointed to a sign on the tunnel wall. It read: Howard's Circus Emporium. It seemed that each creature passing along was required to present an interesting gift for the circus gate keeper; no gift and you die...

"I'll look in my sack for something Jane, here goes..." The Professor pulled out two tablets. "Which one do you want this one or this one?"

"What's the difference?"

"Look! Just have that one then." I noticed that he had thrown a slightly smaller one towards me, would it matter?

"Thanks... I think." I picked it up and licked it, but as I didn't think of anything it didn't change at all!

As we walked along the sewer, past the sign, we saw a strange little creature. He had big rubbery lips and a cheeky smile; he also spoke in a dialect that I had never heard before. He seemed to rush his words; we didn't understand what he was saying at all.

"Blaaa! Blaaa! Gift! Blaa! Blaaa!" he spluttered. He seemed to grin after speaking. "Blaaaa! Blaaaaaa! Me! Blaaaaa! Blaaaaa!"

The more we stared at him the more his vocal tone became increasingly frantic and more rushed . He grinned again, then he gripped his lower lip with his right paw and squeezed his face. It was odd this. He then sucked at the air creating a deafening whistle that stopped the circus commotion ahead of us...

"SSSQQQQUUEEEAAAAKKKK!!!!"

It made me jump out of my skin. Then we saw a familiar face, it was Jim, "Hello you two."

"Oh it's you," we replied and hugged him.

"Well give him a gift then."

"What did you give him?" I asked.

"Err, that Max-Torch on the Professor's fishing rod, sorry Professor, you can give him anything he doesn't mind, I think."

I licked my small tablet again; I must have been thinking of the mouse's horrible squeak because it changed into a Max-

Whistle. I blew into it to test it out. *Squeak* it went, but it was pleasantly soothing. "Here you are Howard," I said, as I handed it to him. He grinned and let me in. Then I watched as the Professor licked his tablet. His one changed into a Max-Fan. Howard accepted it with glee but snatched the Crimson clothes from him too. He then started fanning us and squeaking on his new Max-Whistle as we went in.

"This way," Jim said, pointing.

"It's very odd here," said the Professor.

"Isn't it just," I replied.

Ahead of us we could see a donkey, a tiger and a seal all performing juggling acts. We could also hear an annoying whistling sound. We turned and saw Howard playing with his new toy. At least it wasn't too loud. But it was beginning to frustrate Jim slightly, so he scampered over towards Howard and made him stop. Howard sulked for a bit and then began waving frantically. What was he up to? It was as though he were signalling towards the roof, but why?

"Well that sorted him out. Ha! Ha! So you left Louis with his roundish thing yeah," smiled Jim.

"Yeah, he's gone quite mad you see," I replied. "It's very odd here Jim, is this the King's X place we seek? It looks very similar to that vision, but I cannot see….. oh wait a minute… over there!" I pointed at an elephant, "that grey beast is on a unicycle, it's definitely similar to that vision."

"It's Oxen Circus. You see without Louis' tricks and a boring regimented route we'd never have found this place."

Suddenly we heard horrible odd cries coming from above us. Then two large black claws snatched Crimson's clothes from the squeaky creature and then grabbed the Professor and he was scooped up and disappeared into the distance. Then another beast flew right past us, it was an evil looking crow and Jim said it wasn't a crow at all, it was a raven. We then began to hear mumbling inside the tent saying that the new mice will be taken to the seven towers. Was that us? Suddenly two more big claws appeared and then another two. We were grabbed and hung, upside down like before. The beasts in the air spoke of food and how they enjoyed fresh mice.

"Oh Jim! Jim! We're going to die and that's exactly what Louis told us might happen. He said that unless you catch that hope-moth you'd be a goner and as we're with you, so will we!"

"But I caught the moth Jane, and it's still alive, see." Jim opened his left paw and showed me it. "I don't know what to do with it but I've got it."

5. Disguise was Wise

The following chapters were taken from Louis' personal notes.

As first Jim, then the Professor and Jane, vanished into the blackness, I cursed them for being traitors, while I sat alone with the round object on the King's X higher level. I was still sitting by the edge of the hole crying when a young, earringless unpredictable walked up and sat next to me. This unpredictable did however wear one of those wrist things and it read 11:40a.m. This gave me just 20 minutes to find Ken and negotiate a deal.

I was sitting there mumbling to myself, a common trait in mice when they are alone. "Typical.. selfish ..mice....no good... no...faith....no hope.....Wait!"

I suddenly remembered that in the Sacred Scrolls there are three great words: Faith, Hope and Charity. In order to fulfil the third section of the sacred words I must try to help my friends for, although they had deserted me, they had been blind to the truth through no fault of their own other than inexperience and ignorance. I sat there thinking about my friends and how their foolishness was purely a result of their lack of knowledge and their naivety.

Blindness is such a common disease when your eyes are closed to the world. But if they could just open them and see the bigger picture then, like me, they would see things differently. My friends took what they had for granted. They didn't realise that without following a chosen plan their ideas would become mixed. But without them, I myself was a nobody. What is the point of existing if the friends I trust ignore me. I need to earn trust, commitment and respect. Yes! If I am to be the ONE I must solve this riddle, the biggest most complicated riddle of all, the answer to life's ultimate question: why am I here?

"Help me!" I shouted (actually more squeaked) towards the small unpredictable. He responded and helped me carry the roundish thing to the main entrance. Now I had a choice: was I to go left onto the road or right to a station. It was called St. Pancreas.

The unpredictable bent down towards me and pointed to two hamsters at the St. Pancreas place. We struggled over, still carrying the roundish object. Then the little unpredictable smiled and asked me a question, "Why are you carrying a wooden chopping board, silly little mouse? Do you want to cut up some cheese? Is that why?"

Suddenly I heard loud, argumentative voices. The unpredictable turned to me and said, "That's my parents, I have to go, good luck with those hamsters!" he then smiled again and left.

I understand now that not all unpredictables are bad creatures and I am sure that if he tells his family they won't believe that he spoke to me, a small fluffy mouse, carrying a roundish chopping board, on roller skates; which is good, I think. I looked down and saw one of MacDrid's tablets stuck to a sticky thing on the roundish table. I licked it and thought of a hamster mask and put it on.

I arrived alone, wheeling along the roundish object. Ken was there, as was a pecan nut and Andrew Archdeacon. Fortune though was on my side as I was wearing MacDrid's cloak by accident. I didn't remember putting it on at all... oh hang on... when I was deserted I had put it on because I was upset. I remember now. Maybe this is what the Sacred Scrolls meant when they said that certain things will be discovered by fate?

The hamsters looked well fed and I spoke first. I attempted an accent although you could have told it was me under there if you'd known me. "Hello guys, we meet again."

"I saw you last week, didn't you get my note? I sent my best raven and he said your castle was on fire... what happened? Anyway, I'm meant to be meeting some mice, but well, nice to see you," answered Ken. "I don't suppose you brought me anything, did you?"

"Yes! I brought the secret to everything, this..." I rolled out the roundish thing. The small unpredictable had said it was a chopping board but I didn't know what that was so I had the fingers of my left paw crossed. Was this what the Sacred Scrolls meant by living dangerously? We opened it and a bit of cheese rolled off and Andrew gobbled it up straight away.

"Yummy," he grinned, "it's a table, an odd table."

"Cousin, I thought you were dead," I said.

"Oh no! No one can kill me unless they cover my soul with living dust. It is a riddle from the Ssssylfia from many years ago. I cannot die MacDrid, unless you can locate my soul and finish me with the living dust."

"Is the *ONE* the dust or is Richard the *ONE*?"

"Neither MacDrid, poor, silly MacDrid," snapped Andrew.

"As it's still morning let's wait for a few more minutes, you see I'm expecting some mice to arrive at noon," muttered Ken.

"Cousin," said Andrew, "if they don't come we must go to my tower, I would like to show you my plans. Ken, you may bring that pecan, I did that to him, he double-crossed me see. Two Name decided to side with mice and rats. I couldn't believe it. What kind of hamster sides with mice and rats?"

"These mice I'm meeting have the Rodent Key," grinned Ken, "unless that traitor known as Crimson Pigs has still got it. You see, Crimson impersonated my comrade RedBush and stole the key from my grasp and no doubt he's been to the faith safe too."

"I've met those mice, at my castle, a funny one in a crimson hat and a female. And I captured the tubby one but he escaped with the Rodent Key," I replied. (I was somehow getting away with my disguise, which was a relief).

6. Oval Visions

"Escaped, interesting. But pray tell, why did you bring me this odd table with these funny engravings?" asked Ken. I was beginning to worry that he was working out that I wasn't really his cousin. After all MacDrid was old. I decided I should try a new tactic and sit on the floor. Yes, maybe if I said I was feeling weak and too old to chat all day, then maybe my subterfuge would succeed.

Andrew seemed worried though. "We need that key you fool, as we also need the magical liquid from the bottle at WaterLoo. This Rodent Key opens the faith safe. That's all it does. Yet if we take some of the magical liquid to my towers we may find the secret to the *ONE*. The pecan traitor Two Name is our guinea pig you see. We'll test it out on him. If he dies, so be it! But we need the liquid!. We must have the liquid!"

"Wait!" I squeaked, "Look at the table, the engravings are moving and it's turning misty."

We all watched as a pattern and a vision emerged on the table. At first it turned into a cloud of grey mist and then into a moving image.

Suddenly, as the mist cleared, three ravens were revealed heading towards the seven towers. Each raven was carrying a rodent. The raven on the left held a basket with a crimson hat, scarf and RedBush's locket.

"That's Crimson! But where's the Rodent Key? Wait... maybe his locket no longer holds tea, maybe he replaced it with the key?"

Ken stroked his paws against the engraved marking on the table and a magical mist hovered above the disguised Professor, enlarging him to fill the frame. Suddenly the locket became transparent and inside we could see a red liquid.

"What kind of liquid is it?" I asked.

"It's the magical juice discovered by Lyndon," smirked Andrew. "He was a hamster and the creator of the Sacred Scrolls. He used water to control the electric currents. And electricity is the future. Some mice believe Jerbil MacTaggart wrote the Scrolls. They think hamsters aren't included, but they're wrong. Lyndon believed that the ONE must be a hamster. Not an ordinary one though, a special ONE. ONE that would be able to understand the Dark Energy that eludes us all. You see, DM is common but DE is not. If we solve this riddle then my plan, I mean our plan, to control the world will be possible."

"So Crimson has the liquid in the locket, good," said Ken.

"Yes, and my ravens are delivering him straight to me... Ha! Ha!" laughed Andrew.

"So how do we get to your towers?" I asked.

"Well MacDrid, you and Ken must join me on a magical trip." Andrew was holding a brown leather bag. He pulled out a large platform. Attached to the top was a handle. He clicked his fingers and out of nowhere an enormous raven arrived. We all boarded. Ken carried a pecan behind him and myself and Andrew clamped the roundish table onto the edge. Andrew again clicked his fingers and the raven hoisted us way into the air and in the direction of his seven towers.

"My towers are on a hill, look, can see you them over there?" He pointed to the seven towers. They were next to a watery river and a concrete river. The towers can change appearance when viewed from different angles. There is however an eighth tower, my Awful Tower, but that's my secret place and not even you MacDrid will be told of its location.

"Your castle seems nicer than mine. All I have is a silver cube guarded by elephants and crows; what guards do you have?" I asked.

"My guards are those odd looking unpredictables. I call them Beefeaters. If any cow or oxen tries to break through my defences they will be eaten you see. I own a circus in the centre of town, and the cows and oxen are plentiful there and know that if they double-cross me I'll feed them to the Beefeaters!"

"Is that where those mice were caught?" asked Ken.

"It must be! You see, my ravens patrol the underground tunnels and sewers of London, hunting, visualising, witnessing everything. Without them I'd be as sad as you two. Ha! Ha!"

Andrew was by far the strongest one here. I had to think of a way to solve this riddle. To make Andrew believe Ken was going to be greedy and double-cross him seemed the logical solution. But as I stared down on the city the thought of my friends being alive was the only thing keeping my mind focused...

> Only the *ONE* of pure heart and soul
> will answer many questions and
> discover a new goal…

1. Hamster Secrets

The story continues through Louis' notes…

So Jane, Jim and the Professor had been taken to Andrew's mysterious seven towers by ravens. I had seen them in the vision on the roundish table that we had found at a town called Oval.

Jim chased the hope-moth of light and I fear that his quest would be a failure as nobody has ever managed to keep alive a moth before. I watched as my fellow friends Jane and the Professor deserted me and left me in the hands of, dare I say it, the unscrupulous Archdeacon brothers. I am pretty sure now that they didn't mean to and maybe my mistake was in not following them after all.

I met with the Archdeacon brothers at King's X after I was assisted, amazingly, by a young unpredictable who spoke to me and understood my pain. I, somewhat by luck rather than judgement, disguised myself in MacDrid's cloak and the hamsters believed I was their cousin. I learned from them that their hamster forefather, Lyndon wrote the Sacred Scrolls but through their sneaky behaviour they have convinced the whole rodent population that they were written by Jerbil MacTaggart, a crossbred gerbil and jerboa. I knew nothing about this Lyndon except that he used water with electricity. Was this how the now deceased MacDrid had managed to control Jim and then the Professor at the Faraway Castle?

Andrew seemed to believe that Jerbil MacTaggart was a fantasy being. A guise set up by Lyndon to fool other rodents into believing made up scrolls and possibly made up Rat-Routes.

I was uncertain as to our future more than ever now. I really believed Jerbil MacTaggart was real. Bizarrely Jim never did. Jim suggested, even back in our sawdust prison, that Jerbil MacTaggart was Scottish- oh how could I have been so blind as to question him?

Is the potion that makes Dark Matter the real jewel in this world's crown? What are the tablets, that these hamsters and my friend the Professor use, really made of? Is the constitution of these very tablets relevant? Why do they need to be licked? I too have tasted the tablets and used my imagination to create a wonder of ideas. I remember that when I tasted them I felt a tingling sensation on my tongue. Was this a reaction to the energy that flows inside me? When I licked them I felt a spark of electricity; was this relevant? What kind of substance do these tablets need to be for me to have a reaction like that? The Professor has never discussed how the tablets work. Did he really invent them? I think not. I believe they are taken from the tablet jars at that whiskered unpredictable's library near WaterLoo. I believe that Crimson, the crossbreed stole them from that unpredictable's lair. I believe that the Archdeacon brothers have also stolen from the unpredictable's lair. Was it not in the faith safe that they found the magical juices in the bottle of WaterLoo. And was it not me, a mouse, that captured this liquid in the locket of our fallen hero Crimson? And was it not the Professor who was wearing this locket around his neck? And was it not the evil Archdeacon brother's plan to take it from him for their own personal goals?

I believe that the Dark Energy that we have been searching for is really our emotions, our imagination and our instincts. There must be a reason why, when we sleep we recharge ourselves, and awake with an accelerated energy. An energy that isn't visible yet is all around and inside us. My instinct, my Dark Energy, told me that our conflict with the hamsters was far from over.

As a group, from that sawdust prison, we had come so far, yet as individuals we might progress further. I, alone and in disguise, was negotiating with the hamsters. As a group, Jane, Jim and the Professor had been ambushed and caught. As an individual, Eon had joined a new group with other types of rodents and dare I say it, less than scary scratchers. I had seen Jim worshipped in his own dreams, and by a round faces. I had met Crimson, and only through his lack of communication and teamwork did he die. I had seen the Collective hamsters, not as an army, but only in small groups; is this relevant? If I go to Scotland will I find a town under military hamster control? Will all the other mice just be pecan nuts, changed by the madness of a greedy hamster? As a group we had come so far and we will be reunited. Albeit reunited in a world run by hamsters. How long will this world be an unpleasant land?

Jane told me once that Jim met with a bee that wore knee pads inside a chocolate machine. The bee was called Velocity, but surely Velocity means fast? How can a young bee talk, let alone be fast? This bee came to light in one of Jim's exaggerated stories, but maybe in a bizarre Jim-like way what he says is true. Maybe Velocity was a new kind of sign from the mysterious Ssssylfia. Maybe Velocity was an unknown force that will ultimately assist us in our reasoning with these plotting hamsters. Maybe Velocity will be a power for victory in the salvation of all rodent kind?

I was still in disguise as MacDrid and hoped I wouldn't blow my cover as it could quite easily end my life. The raven carrying myself, the pecan and the hamsters arrived at one of the seven towers. It was situated on an island. Andrew and Ken started giggling and I wasn't sure what to make of it, so I joined in. We climbed off the platform together and followed Andrew to his front door.

"Is there anybody there?" asked Andrew, knocking on this tower's door and his raven, in the silence, sat on the grass of the tower's ferny floor. Then the beast flew up to a turret, way above Andrew's head. Andrew knocked on the door a second time, "is there anybody there?" he said.

"Andrew! Andrew! Who runs the place when you're not here?" asked Ken.

"Oh, I don't trust too many beasts but I've found one loyal friend, he's a mouse actually, named Eon. I met him in a town called High Gate. I think he clunked his head in a battle with a scratcher, as he seems to have lost his memory. I told him we've always been friends and he believes me. He's very tough.... look, here he comes." Andrew pointed at Eon as he opened the door. He was slightly hunched in posture, had swirly eyes and wore a large silver headband.

"I used headbands on my victims too," I said to Andrew.

"Yes I've heard you did," he replied. "Hang on, where are you off to?"

"I need a rest. I am old and need a lie down; my old bones seize up when I stand too long and holding onto that pie was uncomfortable. You go inside, I'll join you in a little while." I told a white lie as I needed to consult the Ssssylfia if I was to defeat these hamsters. Part of my pretence was to use MacDrid's ailing health. I needed to act cool and pretend everything was fine but still be unwell and old.

"Okay then MacDrid, I understand. When you're ready then. I've got so much to show you and Ken."

I waited for the babbling hamsters to disappear into one of the rooms and I rushed towards the higher level tracks at Towers' Hill...

I thought Towers' Hill was a silly name as everyone who goes there can see all the seven towers on a hill. I scampered down the steps and met with a tremendous shock. This mechanical beast was on a different line. A tunnel that circles London. It was scary. I recognised only King's X from my Black line exploits. I knew the great legends of other tunnels but I never thought them to be true. On the wall beside me there was a vast unpredictable map. It listed about ten different lines spanning the whole of London. There were quite a few stations linked to Ken like South Ken, High St Ken, Kensal

Green and others to parks and commons. I couldn't believe there could be so many. It would take me a whole lifetime to explore them all. The others, Jim, Jane and the Professor would really think I was mad if I showed them this. Then I noticed High Gate's sign and thought of Eon. My friend Eon, who was now under the control of the evil Andrew. Images of our fun together reflected in my thoughts until an ear-ringed unpredictable almost crushed me with her left boot as she was boarding the mechanical beast. As it left I waited for the Ssssylfia. I needed one last riddle to help me save my friends from certain death. As if on cue, as the mechanical beast disappeared into the blackness, I saw her drift towards me.

> Just like the rodents of ancient times,
> You strive to read these sacred signs
> Of all whose hearts long to feel the moment strike,
> Yet you need to help them taste the passion
> As if it were their first real ration,
> Their first real flavour of everything...

Think to yourself Louis, what does it mean? I must read the logic in its lines. To understand the simple things. If I become irritated then I will become agitated. It spoke of the rodents of ancient times. I believe it is asking me to teach my friends the way of the world because I know what's happening. I must lead them to victory. It said that inside their hearts they long for my help, yet if I allow their arrogance and greed to get in the way we will surely fail. But why did this Ssssylfia say such things to me I wonder? Was the Ssssylfia the *ONE* we seek? If she was then we'd already found it. Suddenly she spoke again:

> JIM HOLDS THE KEY TO UNLOCK THE TRAPS SUCCESS DEPENDS ON UNDERSTANDING THE MAPS

What did that mean? What was it trying to say to me? Andrew had said the *ONE* was a pure rodent, not a crossbreed;

but whenever we really needed help Jim had been there. Was he the ONE I wondered? He was a lucky mouse, so maybe he was...

Yes! If Jim was still alive and had managed to capture the hope-moth which was the light of hope, then maybe he is the ONE! Ssssylfia speaks of him holding the key to unlock the traps. What traps were these I wondered? And our success depends on understanding the maps, what maps? The unpredictable maps or a map connected with Andrew? I wondered if Andrew could be fool enough to show me plans of his towers, only time would tell...

I rushed back up the hill to the towers. I donned my MacDrid cloak again and calmly walked to the door of the closest one. I was about to knock when I noticed it was slightly ajar. I pushed it and entered. Inside there was a beautiful hallway, it led to a stunning marble staircase; was this the same tower as before? It looked different somehow.

I could hear a faint chomping sound coming from above me, so I scampered up the stairs where I discovered a large oak panelled room. All along the edges were the stuffed heads of animals. Andrew had the usual things, deer, bears, tigers, lions but I also saw a decapitated rodent. It looked like Jerbil MacTaggart. The jerboa who had spoken of freedom for all of us. My God, what had they done to him? His head and body were linked by metal wires. His head was on a spike and his body was attached to a large machine across the hall. A trickle of electricity rippled inside this machine and now and again his body twitched. Were they bringing the headless corpse back to life? As I stared at the machine I heard footsteps, I turned to see Andrew and Ken walk in.

"Hello MacDrid," Andrew said, "I'm so glad you could make it. I was getting a little worried there. Oh yeah, do you remember Ken telling us he was gonna meet four mice at King's X? Well look up there," he pointed to my friends who were imprisoned in individual cages. "That's three of them."

"They're the mice from the vision on that table you brought me," said Ken, "and, this MacDrid," he scooped out a paw-full of liquid and flicked his fingers towards the pecan, "is the magical liquid from the locket."

"Look at the pecan!" Andrew squeaked. As the drops of liquid came into contact with the pecan they caused it to break open, and out popped a rodent. It looked like Max's stepbrother Paul, who I'd played cricket catching against all those months ago.

"Paul! Paul! Up here!" yelled the Professor.

"Max, is that you?"

"Yes Paul! Yes!"

"What's happening?" asked Paul, "Andrew, why are we in your tower and not at your end-of-the-tracks kitchen?"

"Well, that's because circumstances have changed. RAVEN! Take this rodent and put him up there." Andrew pointed to the cage next to Paul's stepbrother, the Professor.

It was surreal how identical they looked. How could Paul be a crossbreed when he looked so much like the Professor? Then a nasty thought struck me, maybe Max was a crossbreed too, that would explain everything...

"You'll never get away with this, none of you..." Paul stared at me and winked. I realised that he must have known that I wasn't the real MacDrid; then suddenly a huge raven grabbed him and hoisted him away.

"I never did like that two-name rodent. I didn't know whether to call him a mouse or a hamster or indeed by his name Paul or Richard or both," snapped Ken.

"Nor me," grumped Andrew. I just kept quiet. It is written that if you have nothing to say, say nothing.

"So what's your plan Andrew?" asked Ken.

We were all sitting at a large table drinking, and eating pecan pie. I ate just the crust as I wasn't keen on being a cannibal. Andrew's favourite raven was allowed to eat with us, as was Eon, but sadly my friend didn't recognise me at all. I considered whacking him across the head in an effort to wake him up, but thought better of it. As for the raven, he was a lot smarter than any of the real MacDrid's crows. But as time drifted on I knew I had to act as Andrew seemed to want me to talk of an experience from our youth together, and since I wasn't the real MacDrid it would've been a tad complicated.

"I'm gonna take a wander around, have you got any maps at all?" I asked Andrew.

"Sure I have cousin." He passed me a large in depth map of the tower and surrounding court area. He said there were seven towers and I had free access to them all, except the Awful Tower. This awful one was his own private place. Not even his best raven was allowed there apparently. I scampered off. Really I wanted to free my friends but, at this point their escape was the least of my problems. I remember walking around a corner by a large set of steps, then everything went black. Someone or something had grabbed me from behind and thrown me into a black bag. It was air tight so I found it difficult to breathe until suddenly a knife sliced into it. It grazed my fluffy face leaving me with a deep cut near my left eye. All I remember was being clunked on the head and then waking up in a dungeon.

"Louis! Hey is that you Louis?" I could hear a voice but I was gagged and blindfolded.

"It is you isn't it? Why didn't you say before we grabbed you? Jane, untie his bonds and release him," said the voice.

She cut the ropes around my paws and removed the black bag. She removed my mask, we hugged and she led me to the others.

2.

The Traitor

Once again, Jane takes up the story...

"Louis, it is you," squeaked Jim and he rushed over and they hugged. "Am I glad to see you. But why are you dressed in MacDrid's cloak? And why is Andrew still alive? Did you see Paul? He's trapped up there with the Professor, look," Jim pointed to the two stepbrothers and they looked almost identical.

"The fact that Andrew's still alive is of great concern," sighed Louis. "So many things have happened since you disappeared. I've seen so much. Luckily though, Andrew and Ken believe I'm MacDrid. As for Andrew, there is only one way to kill him, he won't die by any natural means. We need to find something called *'living dust'*. His soul is, I believe, in a secret place known as the Awful Tower. It's the tower we saw in that vision ages ago. We need to find this living dust and scatter it over his soul in order to destroy him. As for the *ONE*, Andrew believes it is a pure breed, but not a mouse; unfortunately it's location still eludes us."

"That sounds complicated Louis," said Jim.

"That's because life was never meant to be easy."

"Jane says that you thought I should be dead, why?" asked Jim.

"The moth is a symbol of light and of death, creatures of the blackness which only appear at night. If a moth flutters and tempts us to it, unless we can capture it, we will die."

"Is that a true story?" asked a worried Jim.

"It is written that dead rodents tell no tales. This tale originates from the dying words of the legend himself."

"Well it doesn't matter as I caught that moth, see..." Jim reached into his pocket and then opened his left paw and there was the moth. It left a powdering of dust in his pocket. "Wait! It sheds dust! It is alive and sheds dust, it is the producer of living dust!"

"Yes! We must use this to destroy Andrew, but now is not the time," whispered Louis. He started to get agitated, as though we were being watched. "Jane, ask the Professor and Paul to join us in the eleventh cannon in five minutes, we need to plan our attack..."

I watched as Louis and Jim scampered towards the dungeon. But why the eleventh cannon? What was the significance? Meanwhile the Professor and Paul were becoming acquainted again. The Professor had escaped using a Max-Rope and then threw it to Paul. I saw them both chatting near the large marble staircase, in full view of Andrew and Ken; if either of them raised their heads from their dinner plates they would be captured for sure…

"Pssst! Hey, you two, over here." I attracted their attention and guided them over towards me.

"What?" squeaked Paul.

"Shhhh! Not so loud," I whispered.

"What do you want?" whispered the Professor.

"Louis and Jim have a plan for an escape, we need to meet them in the eleventh cannon now."

"What, right now?" asked Paul. Strangely he seemed reluctant to go. He appeared to be stalling and this did not instil feelings of trust; I was wary.

"Never mind," I said. I scurried back to the others alone.

"So where are they?" asked Jim.

"I think it's a trap. Paul is acting odd so I left him with the Professor."

"A trap?" Louis scampered slowly up the stairs followed closely by myself and Jim. Sure enough we saw Paul talking with Andrew and Ken. They called him Two-Name and suddenly our hearts were in our mouths; this traitor was Max's own stepbrother! We saw that the Professor's sack of inventions was on the table in front of them; but where was Max? We looked up to the cages but he wasn't there. Then we noticed a large raven flying off in the distance carrying a small basket. Could the Professor be in this basket? Had he been double-crossed by his own stepbrother? Louis decided something needed to be done.

SADNESS! PAUL'S A TRAITOR

"There's so much to do and yet so little time," whispered Louis. "Friend's, the time has come to rid the world of these hamsters forever. If we can destroy Andrew then the ravens will panic, Ken will panic and we'll be able to escape. I alone will take the moth to the Awful Tower. Jane you climb up there," he pointed towards a ledge. "That will be a good lookout point. You will have to signal to myself and Jim when the coast is clear, that is when Andrew, Paul and Ken are facing the other way. Then, when we're safely through I need you to grab

Eon and lead him to the eleventh cannon. Lie to him to make him follow you."

"What am I doing?" asked Jim.

"You need to rescue the Professor. Have you got a Max-Rope?"

"Err, yes."

"Good! Off you go then, you have no time to lose. I'll meet all of you by the eleventh cannon on the left in thirty minutes, clear?"

"Umm, how, exactly, do I rescue the Professor? Have you got a plan or do you want me to make it up?"

"Make it up Jim. Use your initiative. Remember that simple solutions are always available. Don't try to be too clever. Use your brain and work on instinct. If you think of an idea that sounds possible do it straight away. Don't let doubt creep into your mind. Doubt is the one thing that could result in your death."

"But why can't I do the moth job? I caught it and after all I've got it, see..." Jim showed it to Louis who in turn grabbed it from his fluffy paw.

"Shhhh! Jim, we don't have much time, just believe in yourself."

"Great, thanks for nothing.....Oh well....great," mumbled Jim and he sadly sloped off on his own.

3. The *ONE* Revealed

I climbed up to the ledge using a Max-Rope. When the two hamsters and two name were picking up their plates and licking the remnants from them, I gave the signal.

Louis ran right and Jim ran left. I had quite a good view of both towers. Louis reached his first. I watched as he picked at the door with a Max-Crow-Bar (I guess he had popped it in his pocket earlier). After he opened it he rushed inside. There were little windows running up the entire height of this tower. I guess it had one window per floor. I couldn't see Louis properly but every now and then I glimpsed a hind leg, or his fluffy face, or clasped left paw through the glass. But the higher he went the harder it was for me to make him out. I remember blinking both my eyes simultaneously and then he was gone. I looked up and down the tower but somehow I'd lost him.

Out of the corner of my other eye I was watching Jim. I turned my head fully towards him. He was bumbling along. He seemed to be doing a little skip as he was running. He'd go five steps normally then leap in the air with both feet together. I wondered if he was taking Louis too literally, if that was possible. Ahead of him I saw a ditch filled with grasping paws. Because of his wayward running style he obviously hadn't noticed it. I remember covering my paws over my eyes as he approached it but I guess something inside my mind persuaded me to peek through my fingers. He reached the ditch precisely on his fifth step, and then did his unusual leap clearing the pit of death with inches to spare. Then I saw a sleeping raven twenty yards ahead of him. He went right up to it and seemed to pluck a feather from its tail, then another, and then another and so on and so on. Eventually he had both arms full of feathers but this must have blocked his view because he tripped on a random twig and crashed to the ground. This commotion woke the beast. It turned towards Jim, but as luck would have it he was buried in the feathers and therefore, to the drowsy raven he probably looked like another one of its breed.

It looked to me almost as though Andrew had laid an obstacle course on the route to the Professor. A selection of traps and trip wires. But because of Jim's good fortune, and Louis' advice for him to do whatever came into his head no matter how odd, he seemed to be coping for the moment.

The tower Jim was heading for looked like it was far, far away. It had an odd shimmer to it and floated in the air without any visible support. I watched as Jim suddenly stopped running and tossed the feathers high into the air. The wind the feathers made caused the shimmering castle to shimmer more. Jim ran right up to it. It seemed to me that he pushed his left paw towards a brick at the tower's base.

CLICK!

The brick seemed to suck inwards and a large rolling knife shot out of the main doorway. But how could he have pressed this brick? He was so far away. And how did he know about the rolling knife? He then jumped and dodged in an odd harmony as knives and spears and darts flew at him from all angles. The most bizarre thing here was that his eyes were closed all the time; he was doing everything by instinct. Then I watched as he turned towards Andrew, Paul and Ken and smiled. He started to rummage around in his pocket and pulled out the hazelnut from earlier, or was it the same one? This one looked more like a yo-yo with a large string. I watched as Jim wound it up and then shot it in the direction of the three devious hamsters. It skipped towards them and leaped onto the table. Jim then pulled the Max-Whistle out of his pocket (which I thought I had given to that strange creature at Oxon Circus). How did Jim get that I wondered? Suddenly Jim blew the Max-Whistle and the yo-yo on the table grew in size. He blew it again and it grew again. Both Ken and Andrew tried to grab it. Then Two Name tried but knocked the locket of liquid over it, soaking the yo-yo; the reaction with its spinning surface sprayed Jim in the magical juice. In the confusion Jims' legs turned into great jumping paws and he leaped towards the Professor.

I watched as Jim, still with his eyes closed turned into a jerboa in front of my very eyes and in a flash he grabbed the Professor and they disappeared.

Meanwhile the two hamsters and Two Name were fighting over the odd yo-yo on the table in front of them.

"Look what you've done Two Name you fool," snapped Andrew. He seemed to be attempting to lap up some of the spilled juice, but it evaporated in front of them.

"Why did you do that?" moaned Ken.

"Err, well, you two were fighting over it and I thought…"

"You thought! You thought! You didn't think at all that's the point," squealed Andrew.

"What's happened?" asked Ken.

"I'm not sure, but I think the tubby one might be the ONE," replied Andrew. "You saw him grow great hind paws. He's a jerboa I tell you, like in the rodent legend! He's a jerboa!"

On the table in front of them the yo-yo began to spin slower, as it ran out of power and eventually ceased turning. Two Name grabbed a large plate and tried to smash it into a million pieces, but to no avail.

"Why did you do that?" screamed Ken.

"It's useless, don't you see… that tubby mouse is the ONE, we have to get out of here…."

The yo-yo thing began vibrating in front of them moving to the side of the roundish table where it suddenly produced a silicone tongue. It began to lick metal particles on the engraved writing and then, magically, it changed before their eyes. This strange thing that Jim had found at MacDrid's lair became an oval-shaped mouse with a three foot tail and there, written with its tail, was the word *ELECTRO*. Was this its name?

Out of the corner of my eye I saw Jim and the Professor; in all the hubbub they had escaped. I looked at Jim and his legs were no longer large, he was his normal self again. How did that happen? Did his contact with the magical juice cause a chain reaction with his internal energy? Did his inner thoughts about jumping transform him physically? I looked up and saw Louis scampering along towards me, but he looked sad. Had he failed in his mission?

"Jane! Pssst Jane! Come on, you should have grabbed Eon and met us over there," Louis pointed to the eleventh cannon.

"I couldn't leave, something very odd has happened. Hang on I'm coming down." I slid down my Max-Rope and greeted him. Jim and the Professor saw me climbing down and joined us.

"What's happened?" asked Louis. He wore a familiar confused look on his face.

"Jim's....well...you tell him Jim," I suggested.

"Tell him what?" asked a concerned Jim.

"You know about your legs and that funny mouse…"

"My legs? A funny mouse? What are you talking about?"

"You know… the mouse.. the ELECTRO mouse."

"What?" asked Jim, the Professor and Louis together.

"Did you not see it?" I asked.

"What are you talking about? All I remember is throwing that hazelnut at the hamsters. You see I did the first thing that came into my head. I did what you suggested Louis; everything I did, I did on impulse."

"So you mean you don't know why you blew that Max-Whistle or how your legs grew big." I pointed to the Max-Whistle that was hanging around his neck.

"Big legs? Max-Whistle?" he looked down but he must have lost it whilst rescuing Max. I must've looked a fool, but it was the truth! I do believe that everything he had done, he hadn't thought about. I wished the things that I did, that I didn't think about, could work so well.

"I saw you throw that thing towards the hamsters. You also whispered something at it and…"

But Jim interrupted me in mid conversation, he said "Are you having a laugh Jane? I did throw the hazelnut, but it bounced off the table and I caught it, look, let me show you…"

He began to go through his pockets, he produced some dark feathers, a Max-Rope, a Max-Whistle and a Max-Fan but no hazelnut.

"How did you get that Max-Fan?" moaned the Professor. "I gave that to that odd creature in Oxen Circus. Come to think of it Jane, didn't you give that creature the Max-Whistle too?" he said, pointing at it.

"Yes I did."

"What's the big idea Jim? What going on?" asked the Professor.

"I wish I knew," he muttered. He sat on the floor in front of us and started to rub his eyes in disbelief. "Jane, my friend, please continue with your story."

"It's not a story Jim it's the truth," I yelled, "Anyway I saw Ken and Andrew fighting over this thing then Paul for some unknown reason knocked the locket of juice over it. Well, the magical liquid inside transformed it into a very odd mouse indeed. You see it now has a three foot tail, a ball to move around on instead of feet and two buttons at the front instead of a mouth."

"Is it alive?" asked Louis.

"It seems not. It has the word *ELECTRO* written across it. What do you think that means?"

"I wish I knew Jane," mumbled Louis. He stared over towards the table and watched as the hamsters and Two Name were fighting for the ownership of this strange mouse.

"I also heard Andrew say that he believes Jim is the ONE."

"Why Jim? Why not this strange mouse?" quizzed Louis. He then pointed towards the scrapping hamsters and sighed. "Right those hamsters want that mouse but we can't let them have it, so we'll need to get it from them. We also need to rescue Eon. As for the hope-moth, it died of suffocation in my pocket, therefore its dust did not work on Andrew's soul."

"Do you have a plan of escape Louis?"

"Yes Jim, I do... we need to set a trap to capture these hamsters. I believe we must steal the funny mouse, then use it as bait to lure in the big fish. We must do it by the eleventh hour otherwise Andrew's ravens will see. Fortunately he still believes that when I wear this cloak and mask I am MacDrid, so I therefore need to outwit them one more time."

"But what of my stepbrother Paul?" asked the Professor.

"Until Two Name proves he is worthy of our trust we cannot help him."

"No! No! You can't leave him here with these evil hamsters. I won't permit it." The Professor stormed off in a huff.

"Jim, you'd better watch him, he may blow everything." Jim followed the Professor.

"Jane you go back onto the ledge and when I give you the signal, run, okay."

"Sure, but aren't you gonna tell us the plan?" I asked.

"I would if I wasn't making it up as I went along. But don't worry, when I see an opportunity I shall be ready for it, lock, stock and barrel..."

"Good luck!" I squeaked, and that was the last conversation I had with him for a long time.

Jim had disappeared with the Professor to a dark corner of the courtyard, far from the madding crows (I mean ravens) and I climbed back up my Max-Rope to the ledge from where I'd witness the success or failure of our mission. I guess Louis did look like MacDrid to those hamsters, as they'd probably only vaguely remembered his features. Two Name (Paul) on the other hand, Louis reckoned, would recognise him so maybe he was walking into a trap. Or maybe we should show more respect to him. He was with the hamsters but he looked like Max, so maybe he'd double-cross them too, rather than double-cross us. I really hoped the Professor was right and Paul would be on our side. I watched as Louis slipped MacDrid's cloak and mask on again and walked towards the babbling hamsters.

"What's all this? What are you arguing about?"

"Argh MacDrid! Two Name has only gone and spilt the magical juice all over a mouse," moaned Andrew.

"A mouse?" MacDrid asked.

"Yes, a mouse."

"So?"

"So first of all we thought he'd wasted the juice on that tubby mouse. But for some odd reason this thing on the table has transformed into this bizarre *ELECTRO* mouse," he showed MacDrid the funny little thing with its three foot tail. "And more than that I believe this mouse is the *ONE*, you know, the *ONE*!"

"But Andrew you said the *ONE* had to be pure of heart. I distinctly remember you saying that it couldn't be a mouse," MacDrid retorted.

"Did I?"

"Yeah you did," replied Ken.

"So this mouse is worthless. Let me throw it out for you." I watched as Louis, I mean MacDrid, grabbed *ELECTRO* and popped it in the pocket of his cloak. Unfortunately he picked it up with his left paw.

"How did you do that?" questioned Ken.

"Yeah, how?" queried Andrew.

"What? Do what?" asked MacDrid.

"Andrew! Grab him!" Ken yelled. I watched as Andrew jumped on top of MacDrid. He got him in a body grip and then rolled up MacDrid's left sleeve.

"What's this?" Andrew asked. He pointed towards MacDrid's left paw. "Did it miraculously grow back, is that it?"

"Err, yeah..." Louis mumbled and panicked as he realised his disguise had failed and knew that he had been discovered.

"Ken, pull his cloak off him."

He did what Andrew asked and the mask fell off too and there stood Louis, defrocked. "A mouse eh? A cunning little mouse? You thought you could out smart me did you?" snapped Ken.

"What are you gonna do to me?"

"Ha! Ha! RAVEN!" yelled Andrew, and his largest, most loyal raven flew to the table. "Take this mouse out of my sight. Put him, yes! Ha! Ha! Put him on the eleventh floor of my Awful Tower. Ha! Ha!"

I watched as Louis was hauled away. He just managed to grab the tail of *ELECTRO* before he disappeared into the distance. I guess at least he had it instead of the those three villains. But it seemed the Professor's belief that his stepbrother was on our side was just based on blind love.

"I thought your Awful Tower only had ten floors," said Ken. He looked confused and sad. I believe he was probably more annoyed that Louis had deceived him than that he had snatched ELECTRO.

"That's the point Ken, where is the eleventh floor of a ten floor tower? Ha! Ha! That's why I called it the Awful Tower see, his friends will never find him, not ever. Ha! Ha!"

"What are we to do about ELECTRO?" asked Two Name, "that mouse grabbed it."

"Be patient. If those silly mice try to save him they too will perish. All we need to do is wait. They will try to negotiate a deal sooner or later, then we'll double-cross them and get this mouse into the bargain. A bit like you Paul Richard, a double-crossing two-faced, Two Name spy. Ha! Ha!"

"Can't you just send a raven to get it off him?" asked Ken.

"Where's the fun in that?"

I could hear everything they were saying and I had to tell my friends. I was worried because neither Jim nor the Professor liked Louis that much but I had to ask for their help. I also had to find them first. I climbed back down the Max-Rope and looked for my friends in the belief that they really would help this time.

4. Eon's Reprieve

I saw my other friends by the eleventh cannon outside in the courtyard. Jim was sitting on top of it and the Professor wasn't speaking to him. I felt a gentle breeze against my neck and a cold shiver ran up my spine. I then saw a paw, I was grabbed, gagged and dragged into the dark shadows...

"Shhhh! Jane, I'm okay," said a familiar voice. "It's Eon. I'm working undercover with Paul and some rats. Louis nearly blew everything, but now he's got the ONE we must find him. Paul has been looking for the ONE for several months. It's true he is a spy I'm afraid, but you can't always judge a rodent by its whiskers. That's to say even though he is a spy he's on our side. He told me he has worked with the legendary Crimson Pigs in France."

"But when did you leave High Gate?" I whispered.

"Oh, that was only a decoy you see. A sham. A game if you like. I've been working with Paul and the rats for over a year now. I remember when he left Max at Parker's Piece and blamed Louis. It was all a set up you see. And me befriending Jim, that was a lie too. Jim has the distinct characteristics of the ONE, yet he is not it. It was hard for me to play the part of a stupid mouse when really I was a spy too. You see, we couldn't tell you what was going on, it wouldn't have been correct."

"So you thought it would be better to lie, is that it?"

"Jane I don't expect you to understand straight away."

"So what does Paul want the ONE for?"

"He wants to destroy it. When it was on that table he tried to smash it before it could fully transform. He failed. And now these hamsters understand that if it is destroyed then no evil can come into the world. Don't you see Jane, we're doing this for everyone. The hamsters want to use its power to take over the world, and we want to save the world; but because of Louis' blind meddling the whole scam has been jeopardised."

"But Louis says it's our ticket to freedom. Without it we will never be free. He says we need to discover ourselves to understand the way of the world before we can use this technology. Surely to destroy it would be a mistake?"

"Don't side against me Jane! Don't do it! Here, take the sack of inventions, you'll never rescue Louis without them. And remember, I'm on your side, don't forget that!" I watched as Eon scampered back towards the feasting hamsters.

Suddenly my whole world flashed before my eyes. Louis was the only sane one here yet wasn't trying to be a hero. He was trying to give us hope. I ran back towards Jim and the Professor, they were so caught-up in themselves they hadn't noticed I had been snatched, but fortunately, at least they were now talking…

5.

The Ssssylfia Test

I reached over towards my friends and hugged them. It had been a strange day but it had been necessary.

"Jim! Professor! This is very important to me... listen carefully... Louis has got *ELECTRO* and *ELECTRO* is the *ONE*! Louis' been taken to the Awful Tower over there," I pointed to the bent and twisted tower. The same tower we had seen before in a vision of the future. "A raven has placed him on the eleventh floor and we must save him then get away." Panic was racing from my tongue and I was rambling and rushing my words.

"Jane! Calm down, speak slowly. You say we need to rescue Louis," said the Professor.

"Yes, he's in that tower over there." I pointed to a dark blue tower that had numbers running up its side. Each number represented a floor. It displayed the numbers one to ten.

"Did you say he was on the eleventh floor, how come?" asked Jim.

"That's what Andrew said. I know it sounds puzzling but we must solve this puzzle. Oh yeah, I managed to get your sack of inventions Professor, here you are. Don't ask me how, it's too complicated to explain."

"Oh thanks." I watched as the Professor dipped his paw into his sack, he pulled out a tiny tablet, licked it and it changed into a small pair of Max-Binoculars.

"What are they for?" asked Jim.

"Well, I observed over there a strange sight earlier." He pointed to an unpredictable sign that read Tower Gateway. "This place has overground mechanical beasts. Look carefully and you can just about make them out. Now, I have an a inkling that the Ssssylfia will be around, and if we need a miracle to solve this riddle why not one from the best riddle maker we've ever met. Come a bit closer Jim and try to hold my weight."

I watched as the Professor climbed up the edge of the cannon and then proceeded to climb onto Jim's shoulders, he hoisted his Max-Binoculars to his eyes and waited. Five minutes had passed and Jim was beginning to complain.

"How much longer? Oh, the pain!... can't you remove your smelly feet from my face, you overgrown…"

"Shhh! Jim! I can see it coming…" The Professor started to shuffle around and then quoted the Ssssylfia riddle which was, by far, the strangest one to date.

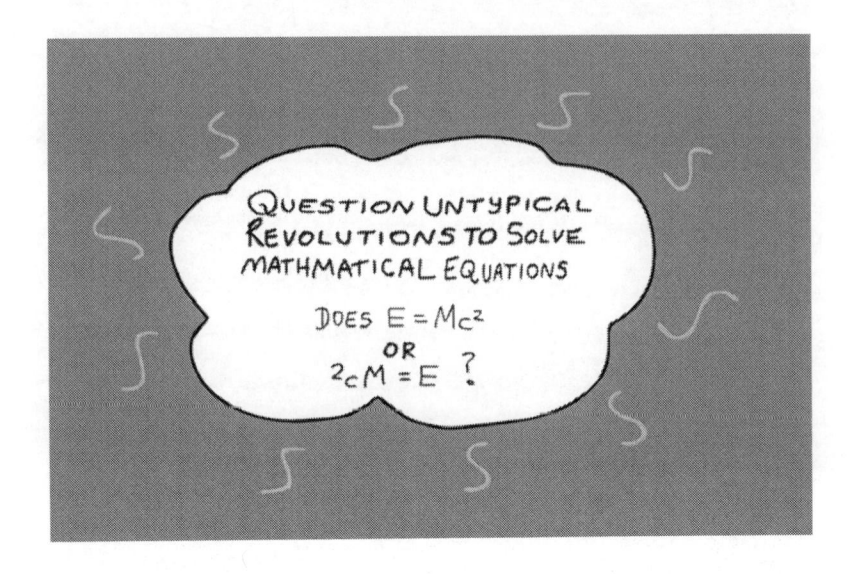

> QUESTION UNTYPICAL
> REVOLUTIONS TO SOLVE
> MATHMATICAL EQUATIONS
>
> DOES $E = Mc^2$
> OR
> $2_cM = E$?

"Well I always knew that would be a stupid idea," moaned Jim.

"Look you must read deep into its wisdom. That's what Louis says isn't it. I think if we understand the bottom line the top two will fall into place. Now $E = mc2$ means what?" I asked.

"I think it means Energy is equal to the Mass multiplied by the Velocity of Light squared," answered the Professor.

"Eh? What do you mean?" I was totally confused by the Professor's mad answer, for although he was a Professor he wasn't the best at explaining things.

"It means that a tiny amount of Matter or Mass if destroyed turns into a phenomenal amount of energy. You know enough to destroy everything Andrew has ever believed in. For example something tiny but significant can create major problems for everyone. Another example would be if you ate the last peanut in the world that peanut could have been planted and produced millions of peanuts, but your thoughtless action would have ruined everything."

"You're always picking on me aren't you," moaned Jim., "you're just like Louis! Maybe he's your blood brother unlike your non-related stepbrother Paul!"

"Stop complaining Jim," I squeaked. "What about the second half of that sentence Professor?"

"That's where we need Jim's answer."

"Eh? Why me?" he groaned.

"Just tell us what you think it means off the top of your head. You see, scientific explanations are discovered either through genius or by luck. The future of our world is riding on your answer, no matter how bizarre," I said.

"Okay.... right... 2cm = E. I think it means two centimetres is equal to, well, eleven," grinned Jim.

"So what does that mean in English?" I asked. I knew Jim's definition would be strange but this strange was stranger than I expected.

"I believe this means that the eleventh floor is two centimetres high."

"So what you're saying is you think Louis must be in the roof, probably in a loft or something."

"Exactly Professor, let's go.'"

"Wait!" I shouted, "what about the first bit?"

"Well it's obvious now isn't it, you said so yourself Jane," smirked Jim, "a spiral staircase in a tower can only spiral up to the top level, this being level ten, yeah. So if Louis is on level eleven the revolution of the steps must be atypical. Therefore he's in the loft."

"But why did the Ssssylfia speak of destroying Andrew?" I asked the Professor.

"I believe that's because we have to do that if we're gonna achieve our ambitions."

"But don't we need to do it now?" I asked.

"No, well, it didn't actually say we need to do it now, did it," answered Jim.

It was funny, before we had heard the last Ssssylfia riddle Jim had been his usual unhappy self, but as he started to believe in himself he became wiser. Suddenly he had almost taken over command. He was definitely a stronger minded mouse now than he had ever been at the start, and his contradictions were just that, mismatched and inconsistent and that's what made him an unpredictable mouse… Oh no! Was this the vision that we had seen in Bell-Sized Park? For wasn't Jim an unpredictable in that vision? I was more confused than ever. I tried not think too much, it was scaring me.

"So are we gonna destroy Andrew now or not? What do you mean?" I asked.

"All Ssssylfia was saying was that it's possible. I reckon the moth's death may have given us another option. But like most things Jane, we don't have to do what the Ssssylfia says do we. We need another moth for that so we'll do it another time. Come on let's go, there's no time to lose."

"Fine." I mumbled and we all scampered away together to find and save our unsung hero, Louis.

6. The Awful Tower

As we journeyed towards the Awful Tower I wondered why it was blue? I remembered that when Crimson Pigs was annoyed he would mumble *SACRED BLEU* under his breathe, was this the inspiration behind his warped thoughts I wondered? But what was the real reason behind the blue walls? The Professor thought it was because Crimson Pigs had been held prisoner there once and was made to blue-wash the walls in Andrew's favourite, dark colour. But whatever the answer was, it wasn't as confusing as the tower's charms. We found some crimson gloves lying on the spiral stairs as we galloped up them and the constant running round and round was making us dizzy. Each level inside was a different colour. Each of the levels had exactly thirty three steps between them. Each step was coloured differently too. No wonder it was called the Awful Tower. Our minds and thoughts were spinning more and more, the higher we climbed. Each step on each level seemed to be more of a struggle. It was probably related partly to the fitness factor. When we all reached the final step we crashed out on the floor. The Professor dipped once more into his sack and pulled out a tablet that I'd seen before. He licked it and it changed into a Max-Step-Ladder. He ran up the steps and began banging against the wood panelling, but we could hear nothing. We could see him really whacking the wood, yet there was no sound; was this another feature of this Awful Tower? A place where there were no sounds. I tried to speak to my friends but only silent words emerged from my lips. We all wanted to say things yet none of us knew how. The Professor again dipped into his sack this time pulling out a tiny tablet. He licked it and it changed into a Max-Screwdriver. He began to undo the screws on the hatch. There were eight screws holding the hinges to the roof. As each one was unscrewed it fell to the ground without a sound. One hit Jim on the leg, drawing blood, and though it seemed in his face that he was whimpering in pain, still there was no sound. The Professor undid the last screw and removed the hatch. He climbed inside, closely followed by Jim and then me. We saw Louis squashed in the corner with his eyes blindfolded. Jim removed the blindfold tape, but strangely, Louis seemed not to notice. It was as though his body was here yet his spirit elsewhere. Louis had his left paw tightly wrapped around the ELECTRO mouse. Even when bound and gagged he had held onto the ONE; he was an inspiration. We carried him down the steps and out onto the courtyard below. Still we couldn't speak, what had happened? Jim pointed up to the sky and we saw that the Moon had eclipsed the Sun. Was this controlling our speech? Was this what was suppressing our voices? Was it a sign from above that we'd outstayed our welcome in this world? As the Moon moved away we saw the Sun again, and the sky was filled with a rainbow. Rain then fell from a scattering of clouds and wonderfully, we heard voices. But our joy was short lived, the hamsters were coming...

"There they are, get them." It was Andrew and Ken. They were charging at us.

"All of you quickly, this way.." Louis shouted. He had a strange presence in his voice, for he no longer sounded like the Louis we knew. He led us to the eleventh cannon. We all followed him into its barrel. Was this his vague plan from earlier when he spoke of a lock, stock and barrel? Inside it was a tunnel. It was as though Louis had known it was there, but how could he have? We couldn't keep our feet stable on the ground as it was so slippery inside. Louis was a long way ahead, Jim and the Professor and myself were lagging behind him. I hoped he was gonna wait for us. I remember looking back and seeing Andrew and Ken both struggling to keep up, their enormous stomachs jamming in the tunnel. Would their greedy eating spree result in them failing to catch us in their very own trap? Or was it they who were trapped? I looked at the walls and saw cabbage leaves and thought of those funny rats. Was this another secret Rat-Route? Suddenly we could see a light ahead and we reached a higher level. It seemed almost as though the mechanical beast was waiting for us, and as we arrived it started to move and we all jumped for the rear bumper. Louis hopped on first, then me, then the Professor, but Jim, on the other paw hadn't made it. Louis reached out and grabbed onto him by his whiskers. I guess if Jim hadn't been so fussy about them before, Louis wouldn't have been able to save his life. As it was though, one did twang before Louis pulled him to safety. Then we all sat on the back of the mechanical beast and Andrew and Ken looked on with dismay. Amazingly we'd escaped...

The Quest Continues...

Links to Hamsterdam and Scotland

"That was a close one Louis, you saved my life, thanks."

"It's okay Jim, that's what friends are for."

"What about Eon and my stepbrother? We can't leave them there with those hamsters," said the Professor.

"There's a lot of things we can or can't do; only you can make up your own mind whether they're worth doing or not."

"But Louis what are you saying?" muttered the Professor.

"If you want us to go back and rescue them then we need to discuss the risks. For unless we understand our own thoughts and dreams we can't even begin to understand the wishes of others..."

"So what now then? You've got the *ONE* haven't you? Do we seek the Dark Energy wall in Bell-Sized Park or what? I really want to see why I was an unpredictable on it," moaned Jim, "or do we try.....oh no! Look at the name of this higher level!" Jim pointed to the name: South Kensington.

"Friends, until we've rid this world of the likes of Andrew and Ken, only then can we pursue our dreams. Jim will you join me?" asked Louis.

"I reckon so, I think."

"How about you Professor?"

"If it's the only way to help my stepbrother and Eon then count me in."

"And Jane, will you go back to the mill and join your seven sisters where you grew up, or join us in another battle for the good of all rodent kind?"

"Louis, so many bizarre things happen when I'm with you, Jim and the Professor. I've got so many questions that need answers, but wouldn't you agree that if I left to go home I would feel unfufilled? Isn't it written in the Sacred Scrolls of Jerboa that the mill cannot grind without the water that is passed?"

"Yes, so?"

"So, I guess my home will always be with you."

THIS JOURNEY AND OUR ADVENTURES ARE BEGINNING TO HAVE A PURPOSE. WE HAVE ALL CHANGED MENTALLY AND PHYSICALLY. OUR DESIRE TO EXPLORE MUST LEAD TO SCOTLAND! ARE YOU WITH ME?

OKAY

BABBLING AS ALWAYS

YES!

"I've got a couple of questions Louis, do you want to hear them?" asked Jim.

"Go on then, but don't tell me Dark Energy is a wall again because it's not, it's our emotions and our instincts. I believe it is the energy that's inside every living creature."

"Well, that's your theory isn't it. So why's your guess- which cannot be proved- any different to mine?"

"Fair point," said Louis, "actually, let's get off here, this higher level looks like it has good hiding places."

We all jumped off and headed towards the blackness by the tracks as Jim continued with his questions.

"Opinions- that's the point init. We all have our own answers as to what Dark Energy is. But, what I'd like to know is what is the *ONE* for, this *ELECTRO* mouse? Why are the rats camouflage specialists? How do rats travel on intergalactic pathways and what are these pathways really? What are the ingredients of the substance in that magical Dark Matter liquid? Why does Jane presume I am a jerboa with big hind paws? I'm not, look at me, I'm like the rest of you. I'm just an ordinary little mouse in an ordinary world. Also why does that Ssssylfia ghost only appear around the mechanical beasts? And what is it? And finally, why do unpredictables control the world not mice?"

"Life can be tough and is filled with so many unanswered questions," sighed Louis.

"You can say that again," we all replied.

Suddenly another riddle emerged from the Ssssylfia.

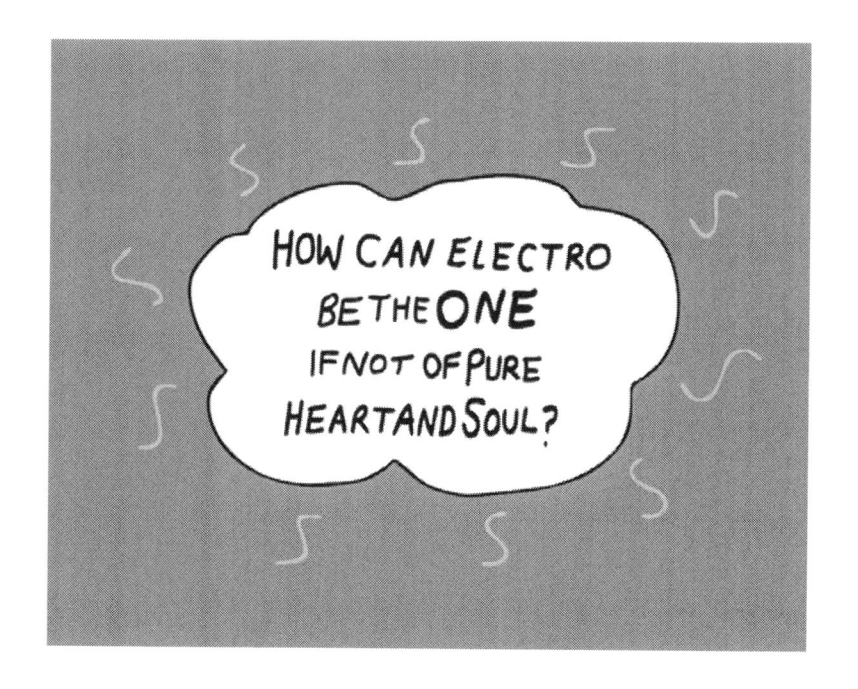

> HOW CAN ELECTRO
> BE THE ONE
> IF NOT OF PURE
> HEART AND SOUL?

"That's been bugging me for ages," moaned Jim.

"Me too," I squeaked. But Louis and Max were silent as Louis was convinced ELECTRO was the ONE and Max's stepbrother, who thought the same, looked more like a traitor than ever before.

"Shall I tell you my theory," asked Jim.

"Maybe tomorrow, it can't be any stranger than today," we all answered.

As we settled down for a nap and wondered about our lost friends and how the hamster's control of London looked worse than ever, the Ssssylfia appeared with one last confusing riddle.

> THE TRUTH LIES WITH THE FOREFATHERS.
>
> BUT DARK MATTER AND THE SEVEN TOWERS WILL EXPLAIN A LOT.
>
> BUT ONLY AT CONSTELLATION 3.14129 WILL YOU UNDERSTAND THE PLOT

"Great, well that made sense, not," moaned Jim.

"Like Louis, and now the Ssssylfia says, we need to go to Scotland and seek out these forefathers," I suggested.

"Good plan, if they are Scottish," said a voice from the blackness.

"That's not Barmy is it?" asked the Professor.

"Yes," he said and he floated towards us on a moving platform. "Go to Scotland if you must, but the real adventures begin across the Great Sea."

As he stopped talking the Ssssylfia appeared once again with two visions of epic proportions. They showed a town called Hamsterdam filled with many horrid hamsters and then a different land, similar to Andrew's with seven towers.

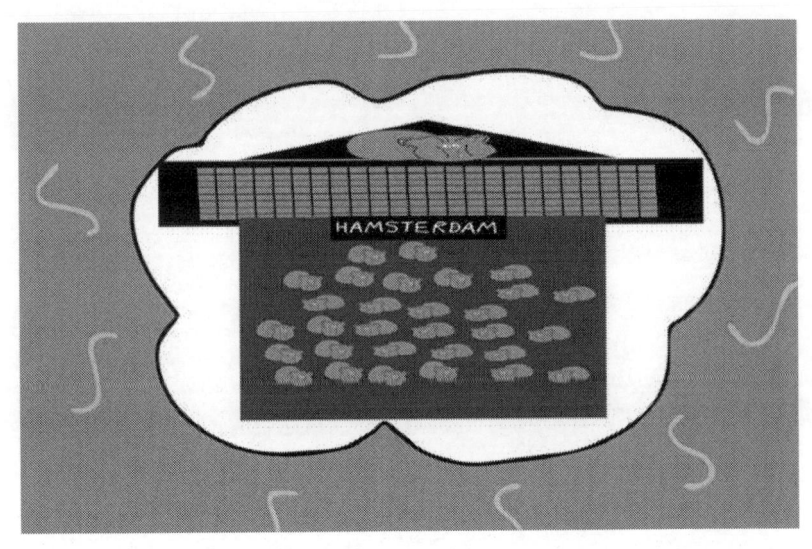

"Look at all those hamsters," squeaked Jim. "I'm not going there!"

"Shhh!" snapped Louis. "Look! Another vision is emerging from the Ssssylfia, I wonder what else we have to watch out for?"

"I know these towers. Let's see shall we," said Barmy, "left to right I think. 1. Hauksbee Tower: it has a static feel, I think. 2. Lyndon Tower and this is run by water. 3. Franklin Tower: that's the spire one; it uses lightning from the sky. 4. Volta Tower: this is for experiments, I believe. 5. Davy Tower: is a pile high and this is used for storage. 6. Faraday Tower: this has magnetic floating abilities. 7. Howard Tower: this is the place where our Rat-Route knowledge came to light. It teaches us to use intergalactic pathways."

"Crazy!" squeaked Jim.

"No, Barmy! By nature and name. Good luck mice in your quest but please cross the Great Sea and hand *ELECTRO* to the European Federation of Rodent's in Hag's Den before you go to Scotland. I think the Ssssylfia is wrong by the way, *ELECTRO* must be the *ONE*!"

"But why do we need to hand in *ELECTRO* at all? We found it so it's ours. And what's it for anyway?" asked Louis, but in a flash, the rat had gone…

To be continued…

In the next 3 volumes Louis discovers he is the *ONE* after all.

The LOUIS THE FURRED series continues circa 2015

Volume Four: The Scottish Forefathers

Volume Five: The Search for Dark Matter

Volume Six: Constellation 3.14129

AJ Howard – Biography

I am from London, England. I gave up my career in advertising after winning a short story competition and this encouraged me to be the writer I am today. I have travelled throughout Europe, hitchhiked in America and been a cruise ship photographer in the Caribbean. I have taken varied career paths since and discovered the real people of this world are down-trodden, lowly paid or work like dogs and these brothers are the influences of my writing style. I am able ability to record, design, illustrate and define any subject in any format.

For more information please follow links to Amazon

fatmousestudios.com

THE ASYLUM YEARS © 1981-2012 is a highly illustrated arrangement of short stories and comic strip adventures.

Many will be made into novels, films or cartoons. My Louis the Furred series started as a three page short story and an updated version is included in this book. My FatMouse character (on my logo) will be seen narrating or treading the boards within this book.

Here are some examples. William the Conkerer: born a horse chestnut, soaked in vinegar and forged in an oven as a baby. There are two Art Gallery comics that teach the power of rational thought and desire. A Slice to Freedom: featuring Dimples, as an optimistic golf ball. Definition Weirdo: a comparison between father and son. No Berries Fool: the berries escape and head for Nonsuch Park because they do not want to be just another yogurt, fool or trifle. The Rhyming Pig-Plant is involved in a Private Investigator Wilmer Wildebeest adventure when Wayne and Craig (the evil pig brothers) steal the crown jewels.

275 pages 50,000 words

| Genre: | Humour / Fiction | Age 16+ |

WARTHOGS © 2010

Amongst the living a leadership of Warthogs terrorise the day makers. With uncanny fixations and complex coded messages they force the weak humans to succumb to slavery. Embittered beliefs that a warrior will save the day the Warthog leader changes into human form to discourage hatred. Incorporating various short stories, the Owl Wizards embark on the salvation of society. Using magic and hallucinations, these nocturnal hunters plot again the regime...

– with illustrations and maps

| Genre: | Fantasy | Age 12+ |

FAT MOUSE PRESENTS series © 2013

Fat Mouse introduces comic strips, puzzles and quizzes for youngsters that assist them to read and spell: No Berries Fool, PIWW, a Slice to Freedom and William the Conkerer are the comic strips. The puzzles consist of Mouse & Hamster code breaking (as featured in the Louis the Furred series) spot the difference and word searches. The quizzes test the kiddies on their understanding of the Bee Confused, the Cream, Louis the Furred and the Wildlife and Run stories.

2 x books

50 pages each

in colour

| Genre: | Humour / Fiction | Age 5-10 |

fatmousestudios.com